Loving

the

Brothers

Pamela R Haynes

Loving the Brothers
By Pamela R Haynes © All Rights Reserved 2018

Edited by Marcia M Publishing House Editorial Team

Published by Marcia M Spence on behalf of Pamela R Haynes

Cover Design: Kevin Williams

Marcia M Publishing House ~ West Bromwich UK B71

All rights reserved 2018

MARCIA M
PUBLISHING HOUSE

www.marciampublishing.com

ISBN-13: 9781999783426

Fiction

Dedicated to my dear friend Amma Rose,

Rest in Peace, Rise in Glory

Loving the Brothers

For my Husband Neville

My Children Jamal, Monique, Fabian, Montell & Patrece

For my Siblings Janette, Andrew, Darren & Lorraine

For my Parents Ronald & Genetha

Special Thanks to my Mentors and Supporters

Dr Ava Eagle Brown

Darren Moxam

Karen Small

Joy, Petra, Carlene, Careen Cheryl D & Valari

Marcia M Spence and the Editorial, Publishing and Design team of Marcia M Publishing House

Readers Reviews

"Hard Punching Tale!"

"A hard-punching tale of three brothers and the women in their lives told from the perspective of the women. Get ready to laugh out loud, gasp in horror, sigh with satisfaction and cry tears during this roller coaster ride of all human emotions. This is an epic first novel from author Pamela Haynes that leaves you wanting more and by Jove, you even get the first few pages of the follow-on book to whet your appetite. A definite 'must read' for 2018."

Cheryl F Deane – London

"Addictive Page Turner!"

"Three brothers, Marcus an accomplished gent, Junior a one-hit wonder and Manley a respected Pastor travel back to Jamaica for their father's funeral. With the late minister Morgan's family all under one roof, three very different women discover that loving the brothers creates water that runs thicker than blood.

Patti, Charmaine and Rose narrate love, deceit and secrets in this compulsive read. The Author Pamela Haynes captures the essence of every single character in this addictive page-turner."

Shelly Allmark – West Midlands

"Highly Impressive First Novel to Savour!"

"Haynes' style is immediately relatable, humorous and above all truthful; a page-turner with a fluidity that weaves the characters' interchangeable lives without any confusion. The book explores the multifaceted relationships and how modern-day London life impacts upon each of them.

This isn't a male bashing book; we see kindness and consideration from Marcus and negative personality traits of the other brothers are viewed in the knowledge that issues that took place in the past often rear their ugly heads and make people behave in highly destructive ways.

The urban reality of London is deliciously compared to the tropical heat and beauty of Jamaica; pulling the reader into the very sights, sounds and scents of the island with vivid long-lasting descriptions.

If there is a negative about the book it is only that one will not want it to end and will leave readers requesting a part two and quickly. A highly impressive first novel to savour"

Joanne Benjamin-Lewis - Birmingham

.

Foreword

Pamela R Haynes knows what she wants, what she stands for and what she will not tolerate!

Her experiences in life have empowered her to live purposefully, to love deeply and pursue her dreams and aspirations passionately.

Loving the Brothers is bold, whilst thrilling. It keeps one in suspense and also inspires. Pamela has a knack for taking the reader on a journey that touches all elements of life and arouses the senses, while looking at the reality of love, relationships and domestic violence. There are moments that Pamela invokes memories in a humorous and an endearing way, a chuckle at the retrospective of innocence and naivety. Pamela skilfully immerses reality into fiction, a stark look at the issues and stigmas surrounding domestic violence. However, there is hope and healing as the book unfolds, giving anyone reading the will to push through any situation they may be facing.

When Pamela read her first chapter two years ago at the Creative Voices event, the audience hung on every word and was left wanting more with great anticipation of the finished book.

I am honoured to present to you Pamela R Haynes, author, future screenwriter and film director.

Pam, I salute you!

Karen Small – Creative and Energy Coach

Loving the Brothers
Pamela R Haynes

One in three women will experience domestic abuse in her lifetime. ~ Refuge

"Nobody is coming to save us!
We have to save ourselves."

Rose Morgan 2015

1 ~ PATTI

I just about caught the 17:10 train from Camden Overground to Stratford Station. Given that the Wednesday rush hour period was in full effect, I was prepared to stand all the way to Westfield, until a young brother motioned to me to sit down in his seat. I didn't argue as my feet were killing me from wearing heels at the office all day.

"Thank you," I said with a smile and hurried awkwardly to trade places with him. He stood over me smiling back and oh, what a smile! All of a sudden, I felt myself blush or was it a hot flush? Difficult to tell at my age; either way, I had to tell myself to calm down. Beads of sweat suddenly formed on my brow as I frantically looked through my huge messenger bag for my fan. All the time this brother was observing me as if I was his entertainment. I couldn't find my fan which I think I must've left in my clutch bag, the one I'd used the previous weekend when I attended a fundraiser at Stoke

Newington Town Hall, for people living with chronic kidney disease. So, I ended up fanning myself with the Metro newspaper that I'd picked up from the station on my way to work. I planned on completing the Sudoku quiz during my break, but I ended up working through lunch. My makeshift fan wasn't working too well so I slipped it back into my bag and undid the belt on my Per Una Mac and the top two buttons on my shirt. I was trying to look anywhere except up!

I looked over to my left; a Polish guy was sitting next to me in his muddy Stone Island tracksuit and an orange high visibility jacket. He looked as though he'd spent the whole day working down a sewer and he smelt like it too. I managed to suppress the bile rising in my throat and quickly looked over to my right. The student in her school uniform sitting next to me was listening to music on her smartphone with a poker-face. In fact, most of the passengers in my carriage appeared to be plugged into one device or another. I don't understand how people can listen to music without reacting in some way. When I listen to music, I want to bop my head, tap my feet, dance or sing-along. I couldn't just sit there. I love listening to music, especially live music. At the moment, I'm on a reggae vibe having seen Chronixx in concert at

Somerset House recently. The concert was so uplifting; I would definitely go and see him perform live again.

Anyway, when I thought 'Mister Man', the gentleman who gave up his seat for me wasn't looking, I took a sneaky peek at him; 6' 4", caramel brown in complexion like a digestive biscuit; medium build, but muscular. The colour of his eyes was obscured by his sunglasses, but I imagined that they were the same light brown as mine. Cute looking, nice goatee and not that much younger than me, I thought. Shoulder length dreadlocks neatly tied back into a loose ponytail. Ralph Lauren T-shirt and probably Ralph Lauren jeans too, which he wore very well. "He most definitely works out," I thought while I observed him as he gripped the rail above with both hands, exposing the bottom end of his six-pack. To avoid looking any lower I quickly looked up at his face and there he was smiling down at me again, like 'something sweet him', I then noticed his gold tooth and instantly lost interest. I winced and thought to myself 'Yes, he's an FOB, Fresh off the Boat!'

I retrieved my paper and started the Sudoku quiz on page 46. The train finally arrived at Stratford Station. I am never in a rush to get off the train; I dipped into my makeup bag reapplied my lipstick and then began searching frantically for my Oyster card. I alighted from the train and plodded along the platform to the escalator. There was no need to rush because I was on time. I always pride myself on being punctual. Stratford Station was packed with commuters. It was late night shopping at Westfield Shopping Centre and there was some sort of sporting event on at the Olympic Park. My feet were 'bunning' me, but I wouldn't be caught dead in flat shoes. I looked forward to meeting my best friend Antoinette for a bit of shopping and a bite to eat. We nicknamed our once a month meeting 'Westfield Wednesday'. It was an opportunity to have a girlie bitch about work, to catch up on the current state of her marriage, my lack of one and to discuss the latest in the saga that was the adoption of their son Elijah, and all this was done over a plate of good food, followed by cocktails at the Sky Bar. It's our once a month treat to ourselves the first Wednesday after payday.

I attempted to walk up the last couple of steps of the escalator when to my shame; I tripped and stepped clean out of my left shoe and watched in slow motion as my good, good Jimmy Choo tumbled down the escalator... right into the hands of 'Mister Man!' Left balancing on one foot feeling embarrassed, my face instantly flushed red, and this time I knew it was no hot flush.

When he reached the top of the escalator, he handed me my shoe and said, "Hi Empress, what's your name? Cinderella?"

My name is a sore subject with me, as I grew up in care, so I was definitely not named after my Grandmothers or after someone important; like the midwife who delivered me. My foster Mother Veronica named me after her favourite soul diva. She was and still is a huge fan so when I tell people my name they always use the same dry line "as in Labelle?"

So, it was amusing to me that when I told 'Mister Man' my name, he didn't flinch and I suspected that it was because he was much younger than me and a FOB so, he'd probably never heard of Patti Labelle! He took off his sunglasses, which confirmed that his eyes were a beautiful light brown. He never broke eye contact as we made small talk, all the time his deliciously smooth Jamaican accent intoxicating me. For the second time that day, I was saying "Thank you." to this stranger.

"My name is Marcus," he told me.

I joked in response, "As in Garvey?"

He laughed a hearty laugh and replied, "Yes, as in Marcus Garvey."

5

Although I protested, he insisted on escorting me to my final destination. Well, there are precisely four escalators between Stratford Station and Westfield Shopping Centre. I was praying hard that I didn't lose my shoe again, trip up, or fall and break my neck between here and there.

Once at my meeting point, we said our goodbyes and he slipped me his business card, which read, Marcus Morgan BSc, Concert Engineer. I watched him turn and disappear quickly into the crowds of shoppers. It wasn't too long before Antoinette arrived. We warmly greeted each other, as we hadn't seen each other since our July meeting. Let 'Westfield Wednesday' begin!

We walked around our favourite shops and ended up at an Italian restaurant in the food hall. We settled into our booth placing our purchases on the seats next to us. An Italian waiter came straight over, but we were not ready to eat, so Antoinette who I affectionately call Ann ordered two glasses of still water. I love Ann and I admire her so much. She's intelligent, beautiful, smart and down to earth. She has an air of sophistication and class about her, which suits her high-profile job as a defence lawyer. Don't let the lace front wig and the Armani suit fool you though, when Ann catches two jokes, she has a disgusting outlandish laugh like a fisherwoman. Mash her toe and she can get ghetto on you in two short steps. Her latest mission is taking on social services in childcare proceedings to legally adopt Elijah. I don't know how they fit it all in, but Ann and her husband Malakai are in the last stages of adopting 4-year-old Elijah, my soon to be godson. He is of African Caribbean parentage; his mother gave him up when he was a newborn baby because she was struggling alone; his is a very similar story to my own. I think Ann and Malakai will make excellent parents and from what Ann tells me, they finally have a court date to make it all official.

The waiter came back with the water and stood impatiently waiting to take our order. Ann told him that we were still not ready yet and he walked away looking annoyed. I prayed to God that Ann wouldn't have to 'wash her mouth on him'. I sipped on my water and filled her in on my job on the 'plantation.'

"Yes," I confirmed that I wore the lemon suit to the job interview. It was the fifth time that I had gone for promotion within my organisation. I work for the Probation Service as a Senior Probation Officer at the Camden Probation Centre. I also confirmed to Ann that I gave a first-class presentation and that I answered all of the people dem questions, just like I did 12 months ago. I could not read the panel members as they were poker-faced and I did not know how well I did either. There were six other candidates and I will know next week. She asked me about the passive-aggressive woman in my team and I told her the woman has seen sense and is retiring in a couple of months' time.

As Ann was about to say something reassuring, the waiter came back and foolishly asked, "Are you two going to order something or what?"

Cue Ann, who retorted at the top of her voice in her Bajan accent "Young man! Right now, you have two things going against you; one you can do nothing about, the other one you can. The first thing going against you is that YOU'RE UGLY but as I said you cannot do anything about that…"

I held my head in my hands… I really didn't know where to look. Aware of the fact that everyone in the restaurant had stopped eating and was now watching us intently. I shook my head in ? embarrassment, disbelief.

2 ~ CHARMAINE

am proper vex! So vex, I can hardly light my bloody cigarette. I've had enough of this shite. It's bad enough that Junior has let me down so many times in the past, but to let the twins down too is so irresponsible! He promised me he would attend the meeting at the twin's nursery this morning and he didn't show up. I had to listen to this woman reel off a catalogue of stunts the twins have been up to and now I'm standing at the number 69 bus stop outside Plaistow Station in the pouring rain. What's the point of being in a marriage when you're doing it all by your flippin' self? If I hear he's been seeing that white woman Mandy again, I'm gonna put him out for sure this time. Well, none of the bus drivers are going to let me on their bus at this time of day with a twin buggy so I might as well walk to Stratford. The only blessing is that the 'Cramp Twins' are fast asleep. Well, after their antics at the nursery, going to sleep is their only option.

"Oh shite!" I shout out loud, stopping at the traffic lights.

Junior going AWOL means I can't do a big shop today in Morrison's and we've got no food indoors. I can't possibly manage the shopping on my own! Where the fuck is Junior and how come he isn't answering his phone? Think Charmaine... ...breathe Charmaine... ...go to Mum's house and she'll sort you out, but don't let her see you so upset; otherwise, you'll have to sit through another one of her sermons!

I love my Mum to the max. She's always there for me and the twins and as soon as I arrive at her home on Pelly Road, with her only grandchildren, she organises hot drinks for us, food for the kids and helps me to dry my hair.

I know she wants to know how the meeting went, but she's patient enough to wait until I'm ready to speak.

Mum fills the silence by watching TV. She loves Phillip Schofield from 'This Morning' and she expertly changes the twins' nappies without once taking her eyes off Phillip. Potty training two three-year-old children has been really stressful, but with Mum's support, the twins are almost dry.

"So, tell me Charms, how did the meeting go?"

And that's when the tears start.

"Oh, Mum it was awful!" are the only words I can utter before Mum crosses the kitchen/diner to give me a cuddle and a shoulder to cry on. She switches the TV to 'The Disney Channel' with the remote control and repositions the buggy so the twins can't see me crying. When I eventually compose myself, I tell her that Gaby and Gary had been roleplaying a fight at nursery during show and tell. Gary was the perpetrator and Gaby was screaming her dad's name and asking for someone to call the police. The staff were obviously concerned enough to call us in for a meeting to check out if things were okay at home. They want me to attend some 'Positive Parenting Programme'.

"The last thing I need is social services snooping into my business Mum!" I sigh "...and Junior didn't even show up for the meeting," I blurt out.

And that's when the sermon starts. To say that my Mum's spirit never took to Junior was an understatement. Mum thought he was the Anti-Christ. The first time they met my Mum was not impressed with his strong Kingstonian accent (even though she's from St Elizabeth in Jamaica herself), or by him having dreadlocks. She also prepared pork for Sunday dinner; despite me telling her that he didn't eat it. Junior stating that eating 'Trenton' was an abomination did not endear him to my Mother either. Yes, the feeling was definitely mutual, they hated each other, and I was bang in the middle of both of them.

He said my Mum treated me like a princess and spoilt the twins rotten. That didn't stop him from eating her food whenever we were short of money! The issue of us marrying so quickly was also something that caused a few problems between us. Mum always felt that although I was expecting the twins, the real reason Junior married me was to get his permanent leave to remain in the UK and she enjoyed bringing it up whenever he was in her orbit.

While Mum went into one, I switched off. All I want now is a cigarette and a container of food to take home for Junior's dinner.

"Charms, are you listening to me?" She asks.

"Yes, Mum," I reply.

"Well, what was the last thing I said then?" She quizzes.

"Yu pick, pick til yu pick shit!" I repeat to her.

Mum sighs and turns back to the stove to fill up the containers with rice, oxtail and butter beans.

God bless the man who invented diazepam! As soon

as the 'gruesome twosome' are in bed I take two tablets with a large glass of 'Lambrini' and I drift off into a lovely deep sleep.

My dream is so vivid; Junior and I are sitting on a beach in Montego Bay. We are sipping 'Bob Marley' cocktails watching our cherubs play games in the sea. We leave 'Gabrielle and Garrison' with their nannies and we walk hand in hand back through the hotel complex to reception. As I check myself out in the many mirrors in the lobby, I am delighted with what I see. I am a size 10 with curves in all the right places. I overhear hubby sharing a naughty joke with the male receptionist and I blush with excitement and anticipation.

After several years of marriage, my husband still adores me, and he only has eyes for me. We kiss like teenagers in front of the bellboy, in the elevator, which takes us up to the penthouse suite. Junior tips the bellboy, who of course wishes he could change places with the successful reggae artist Mr Morgan.

Our suite is awesome with stunning views of Montego Bay from every room. The furnishings are a beautiful tropical palette on a backdrop of coral coloured tiles. The bathroom is breathtaking. Everything is pure white, white tiles, units, towels, white dressing gowns with matching white slippers, white gels, lotions and potions.

We take a luxurious bath together, sipping ice-cold champagne, which the hotel concierge graciously arranged for us while we were at the beach. I suppose it's not every day that your husband's album makes number one on the reggae chart in Jamaica. So, we're making the most of it and celebrating in style.

I love this man to his very core and I'm looking forward to showing him as we have the remainder of the evening to ourselves. The children and their nannies have a suite in another part of the hotel. We will not be interrupted so I take my time to make love to my husband and I savour every moment. We start in the bathroom and end up on the chaise-longue in the bedroom. Junior has an exceptionally beautiful physique, gained from years of clean eating and working out in the gym. I love touching his back and feeling the heat of his body close to mine. While he passionately kisses my neck and squeezes my pert breasts with his hands, I gasp and squeal with delight and begin to gyrate my hips in a clockwise motion.

As if by magic, the first track on Junior's CD (which is about me, of course) is playing through the surround sound stereo system. When he enters me, it feels like the first time; I am so tight, just the way Junior likes it. As he takes me, all I can do is lie back and hold on tight to Junior's shoulders. He then raises my legs over his shoulders in one swift movement and I am getting long deep strokes, which I swear I can feel in my stomach. Junior is breathing heavily like he's climbing a steep hill. He stops briefly to flip me on to my tummy and then enters me from behind. I am screaming my undying love for him as I move skilfully to my knees, arch my back and rock backwards and forwards, backwards and forwards until…

I realise I am not in Jamaica. I'm in Plaistow. I am hot because the heating comes on at 7 am every morning and I am under the duvet. The bed's rocking because 'Dumb and Dumber' are screaming and jumping on my bed and the headboard is banging against the wall! Kiss my teeth! That was just getting good. I move over to the edge of the bed to stop them from stomping on me. I reach over instinctively to Junior's side of the bed but he's not there. In fact, his side of the bed is cold. It dawns on me that Junior did not come home last night. Panic rises in my chest, as this is really unusual for Junior. He may have other women, but he always comes home.

I slowly put my dressing gown on to cover my post-pregnancy body; it is battered from having the twins. Junior was right when he said no man would want me after him.

I go downstairs holding Gabs' hand whilst she navigates the steps. Gary insists on coming down the stairs on his bottom. I have no energy to shout after him as my mind is racing... Where is Junior? He's not in the living room. I open the fridge and his food in Mum's container is untouched. On autopilot, I ask the children what they want for breakfast, even though they always ask for the same thing. I put the cereal into their favourite bowls and warm the milk in a saucepan on the stove. We don't have a microwave because Junior thinks they're toxic. My mind bids me check my mobile which is charging on the kitchen unit. My heart sinks when I see there are six missed calls, but not from Junior, they're from a private number and there's a voicemail message. I listen to the message in the downstairs loo away from the children. Fucking Hell! Junior's been arrested.

3 ~ ROSE

"**A**men and Amen" the congregation declare in unison. I open my eyes to scan the church that is holding its 52nd annual convention in Battersea. Everybody is gathered from Pentecostal churches all over England and Wales. The older church sisters are dressed in their finery with matching shoes, bags and elaborate hats, looking lovely. The menfolk are wearing two or three piece suits and looking mighty fine. I love convention, it's an opportunity to see old friends and make new ones. I love the singing of the mass choirs, the fire and brimstone preaching, culminating in a tearful baptism at the end of the week. I really hope many souls are transformed this weekend as a result.

I became a born-again Christian in 1984 at the tender age of 16, therefore, my walk with the Lord has stemmed over 25 years. In the beginning, my parents were not very supportive of my conversion; we grew up as staunch Catholics. Nevertheless, I led by example and they too converted and became part of the early Pentecostal movement in London in the late 1980s. I stayed at Hackney Pentecostal Church until I got married to Manley, joining him at the Congregation of the Humble Heart Fellowship in Battersea.

Manley and I had a brief courtship; perhaps with hindsight, it was too brief, and very heavily supervised by chaperones. He was the golden boy of his family and everybody was praying that he would follow in his father's footsteps and become a preacher. He was already being groomed as the next motivational preacher in the Pentecostal church and as such, he needed to find a wife. He had to speak to his pastor about courting me and then pastor spoke to my Dad to ask for his approval!

I was so flattered that a man of his stature in the church would even be interested in me. He was so handsome yet so serious, but when he smiled... Lord have his mercy; he lit up the room. We were married six months later and nine months after that I gave birth to our first child, our beautiful daughter Mary, then another girl Martha; two years later. I then had Ruth, Rebecca and Esther. That's right, I have five beautiful daughters. Esther is only six weeks old. I had to have an emergency

C-section due to having high blood pressure, a common but serious condition known as pre-eclampsia. At the final stage of the delivery, I thought that we were both going to die. But thank God for Jesus, because after having the procedure and a blood transfusion I made a full recovery and so did my daughter.

I am here at my first church service since giving birth, to give God all the honour and praise for preserving my life and the life of my little bundle of joy. I am sitting at the front of the church in the first row with my girls. I am dressed in a pale pink linen dress with matching coat, white heels and white hat. My outfit ties in with the pink shirt I chose for Manley to wear. As he takes to the pulpit to deliver this Sunday's service, some sisters in the church need reminding that he's a married man and more importantly, that he is married to me. The Lord has taken us through too much for some woman to get in between us now.

His recent exposure on the church circuit as a newly ordained minister has clearly had a profound effect on improving his confidence. He's walking taller that's for sure. I see it and other women see it too. I sit rocking a sleepy baby Esther in my arms, looking proud as punch over at my girls who look like angels dressed in white summer dresses. Manley proudly introduces Esther to the congregation and cheekily tells them that he's not stopping until he gets a boy. The congregation applaud and I blush holding my head down as I am expected to. My reasons are twofold; firstly, we have not discussed having another child anytime soon. I want to return to my studies at some point to complete my teaching qualifications, with the arrival of Esther; my plans are now on hold again, until she starts school. Secondly, I have not even thought about having sexual relations with my husband again and I definitely am not planning to until way after I have seen the doctor for my six-week health check, which is booked at the surgery for first thing tomorrow morning, actually. I really hope Dr Oko is going to mention family planning and contraception.

I already know Manley's opinion on the matter, which is, "It's all in Jehovah's hands."

But having gone through five pregnancies, I am not that sure I want any more children. In fact, I know I don't want any more children. This has to be a joint decision, but we don't agree. Manley recites from the Bible that a woman should obey her husband but after the close call last time, I fear having another child will kill me and I want to be around for the children I already have! I silently pray wishing that something would happen so Manley is unable to come to the surgery with me tomorrow so that I can talk to my doctor in private about the best contraception for a woman in my situation.

Manley has just read from the book of St John Chapter 1 verse 6, "There was a man sent from God whose name was John."

I straightaway notice the sound effects in the background. The organist is piping in after every couple of words Manley says and the women are shouting 'Hallelujahs' and 'Amens' to fill the gaps. I wouldn't mind but he hasn't really started preaching yet! When did we become so Americanised? Why are people jumping from their pews? Where's the decorum?

In short, Manley is preaching about austerity measures and families going through hard times, "But we are to remain calm and faithful because God has already got a plan and has sent a man to rescue his people from the plans of the enemy. God has already sent a woman…etc. etc." I know this because Manley has rehearsed his sermon with me at every opportunity over the last couple of weeks.

There is more noise and confusion at the back of the church. "Why oh why is this woman running up and down the aisles?" I think to myself. I feel like saying, "If God has sent you a man, he will find you, Sister Carol, no amount of hollering or speaking in tongues is going to speed that up!" Some of these women in the church are so transparent. I get it, they are lonely, and they want to be married.

As one woman in tears told me during a counselling session, "Sister Rose I have so much love to give!"

To which I replied, "...But man's timing and God's timing are not the same!"

Experience tells me when things are not happening quickly enough for us, we force God's hands and when things go wrong, we expect him to deliver us from the very thing we were begging him for in the first place. Sometimes I wish I was still single, footloose and fancy-free, instead of being totally dependent on Manley. Over the years, I have morphed into someone else, a lesser version of myself, a title. I am now Manley's Wife, Pastor's Wife, Mother Morgan, Sister Rose, Choir Mistress, Prayer Warrior, Chief Cook and Bottle Washer. Someone's sick? I am always the one to visit church members in the hospital. No food to eat, my pots are always blazing like a soup kitchen. But who do I call when I need help, advice and support?

I opened up to my Mother once when Manley and I were struggling financially with debts and I was admonished for disrespecting a Pastor in that way. Since then I have kept things to myself. Like the allowance Manley gives me every two weeks and the receipts I have to produce when I purchase clothes for me and the children. The only money that I have access to is the child benefit money. I try to put that away into the girl's bank accounts as a nest egg for their university fees. Sometimes I don't even have money to buy a newspaper or put in the offering plate.

I felt pressured by Manley and my home Pastor, during our marriage guidance course to leave teaching college to support Manley's ministry and then I fell pregnant on our wedding night. People wrongly assume that if you're married to a minister in a church, which tithes, you're set up financially and you're looked after by the church. In reality, we rely on the generosity of a few good people and from occasional love offerings. There are no fancy cars outside our humble home in Battersea, South London.

We only got the deposit for our home when my Uncle Samuel in Jamaica gave us a large amount of money as a wedding present. Little does Manley know, I asked

Uncle Samuel to help us out, as I did not want to start married life living with Manley's parents in Hackney. Manley is so proud; he would be angry with me if he ever found out. I had better not mention the other pots of money my parents have given me throughout our marriage to pay off debts.

I wonder what Elder Jones just whispered in Manley's ear, as he looks very, very shocked? Manley hands the microphone to Elder Jones and then comes the announcement...

Elder Jones advises the congregation that Manley's father Overseer Carlos Morgan has suddenly passed away in Long Bay, Westmoreland, Jamaica following a short illness. I hear a woman screaming loudly at the top of her voice and a heartbeat later, I realise that the woman is me.

We knew Overseer Morgan was gravely ill, in fact, Manley and I had an argument about it a few weeks after Esther was born. I told him to travel to Jamaica to visit his father and he point-blank refused; citing that he could not afford to go. I knew in my spirit that it would be Manley's last opportunity to see his father alive. But he would not budge. I was clear from the beginning that I could manage on my own with the children and I could arrange for my Mother to assist me with the baby.

I was not expecting what came out of Manley's mouth, "Why do you care? He's not your Dad!"

I just bit my tongue, kept my own counsel and went upstairs to pray. The truth of the matter was that his comment really hurt me. Manley's parents were good Christian people, hardworking and honest. They fully embraced me into their family and when they mentioned they were retiring from the ministry and returning home to Jamaica, I cried like they were my own parents. When Manley lacked direction or was discouraged by church politics, it was his parents who offered him guidance. Now, Overseer Morgan also known as Pops Morgan had been called home.

It's a terrible feeling, having to walk on eggshells in your own home, but that's what I do. At home, I quickly change out of my church clothes and begin warming up the food I had made earlier. We normally ate together at the table on Sundays but given the bad news, I decide to feed the girls at the dining room table and fix Manley a tray. Manley is still in his suit sitting in his small study under the stairs; his head in his hands crying, silently. A wave of compassion comes over me, as I place the tray on the desk and drop to my knees to comfort him.

Instinctively he rests his head on my shoulder and sobs his heart out.

I realise in this moment that I have to be the strong one and get him through this. God help me.

4 ~ PATTI

Marcus and I have been dating for twelve weeks and I have gotten to know him a lot better. His parents are Carlos and Kathleen Morgan. The family was raised in Kingston in Jamaica, and his parents now reside on the other side of the island in Long Bay, Negril, in the Parish of Westmoreland. Marcus is the middle son of three brothers; Manley who is married with five children and his younger brother who is married, with twins. It is lovely to hear his family are close and that the concept of marriage is important to him.

I really like being around Marcus and so far, we've been having lots of fun. He has taken the lead in organising our dates and our activities have included romantic meals out, salsa dancing, cinema nights and day trips out in London.

Marcus manages the installation of IT systems at corporate events and concerts. He really enjoys his work as it has given him the opportunity to travel to Europe and the Far East and meet a lot of famous people in the entertainment business.

I haven't been there yet, but I know he has an apartment overlooking the Thames. There's no rush. He hasn't been to my house in Gants Hill either. So far Marcus has been attentive, warm and generous. I do not feel under pressure to do anything and I am relaxed in his company.

The only fly in the ointment is that Marcus is 10 years my junior and whilst he could not care less, I feel a bit odd when we are out and about, and I catch people overtly observing us. To clarify, it's mainly other black women who appear to be mortified by us being together. Hence, I have not introduced him to anyone in my circle yet and my daughter Yolanda only met him briefly when he came to pick me up to go to see Etana at the Roxy.

I have a feeling that my friends would not approve of the age gap and before I met Marcus, I would have probably disapproved as well, hypocritical I know. But it's okay for my friends to be critical, as they have what I crave, husbands who adore and cherish them. As successful as I am, I hate not having a significant other in my life aside from my number one fan Yolanda; and even she's leaving me soon; on her way to university next year, once she passes her 'A' levels.

I was in foster care until I was 18 years old. Fearing I was going to become one of 'Maggie's Millions', my foster Mum Veronica took me to see a career's officer at the Job Centre. I narrowly dodged being put on a YTS scheme and came out with two interviews; one with the British Council and the other with North East Area Probation Service. I took the latter job and after five years in post as a Probation Service Assistant, I won a Home Office sponsorship to study for my degree in Social Work. Although Yolanda was very small I thoroughly enjoyed the course and my placements and I gained, a first-class honours degree from Middlesex University. My Foster Mum, who is originally from Barbados, supported me every step of the way.

I still remember her words of advice when I started university. "Turn up when the people tell ya, sit at the front so you're not distracted and start your assignments as soon as you get them."

She's always had my back and been there for me, even when I fell pregnant with Yolanda at 27 years old. I wasn't a teenage mum, but I would have liked to have been married to her father.

Winston, Yolanda's dad, was a senior police officer with the Metropolitan Police force. A poster boy to encourage more ethnic minorities to join up, but he was already married, with his own family. It was very naive of me to believe he was going to leave his wife and kids for me. When his wife found out about our affair and my pregnancy, to say she hit the roof was an understatement. His wife went ballistic.

The big woman rolled up like a gangster on my doorstep to confront me in the middle of the day, calling me all the names under the sun and telling my neighbours and passers-by what a witch I was breaking up a family home. When I refused to answer the door, she threatened to kick my front door down until I did. To my shame, I didn't behave any better, I was screaming obscenities out of the upstairs bedroom window, telling her to move her Blood Claart and Raas Claart from my door otherwise I would call the police. That comment enraged her even more. She then viciously keyed my car from the bonnet down the side of the driver's door and all the way to the boot. I promptly called the police and got her arrested. It was Winston who persuaded me to drop the charges and after I did, he promptly told me that our relationship was over but that he would support our child. His wife stood by him and they had another child the following year.

Lessons truly learned or as Mum said at the time, "The more the monkey climb, the more he show he tail."

I still don't know what she meant, but on the 24th February 1995, I gave birth to a beautiful baby girl, my daughter Yolanda.

Since Winston, I have been very selective about who I date.

My first question being, "Are you married?"

I have turned down offers from white male colleagues with jungle fever and the one or two black men I met at black networking functions. I found those men to be so arrogant and full of self-importance because they were so few and far between and they thought they were God's gift. Those events were like Speed-Dating and all sorts went down.

I chose instead to focus on raising Yolanda and developing my career. After gaining my degree, I studied for my Masters in Leadership and Management and now I'm in the middle of my PhD. As my employers refused to help me pay towards my studies, they do not deserve to know about my progress. Let them find out when I publish my research in the Probation Journal! In the meantime, I hope I get promotion to the next level. In total, I have tried unsuccessfully for promotion on five previous occasions. I'm tired of listening to and consolidating feedback.

"Well Patti you did not demonstrate the knowledge and breadth of experience required for the post." or "You need to go on a leadership programme for BAME staff, that will raise your profile within the organisation." or "You need a management qualification." or my favourite line, "The other candidate had the edge."

The Edge? What the heck is The Edge? What course do I need to go on to gain that?

I just wish someone simply had the balls to tell me, "Patti, your big ole feet have gone as far as we are going to let them!" or "You're too black to join us up here!"

I simply would not keep banging my head against the concrete ceiling that exists for black middle managers in the workplace. Ann is convinced I am wasting my time there and I should become some highflying lace front wig wearing training consultant, but unlike her, I cannot take the risk and start my own company. Ann has two salaries coming in and I still have several years left on my mortgage.

I sigh, I am sitting on my bed in nothing but my bathrobe having a 'fat moment.' I am going out with

Marcus to the ballet and I haven't got a clue what to wear. He's seen me in most things already. Just as I'm thinking of him, 'Mister Man' rings my mobile on Skype. Without thinking, I answer the call.

"Wha'ppen Empress! A Wah Gwaan?" He hails.

"Hi, Marcus I'm okay you know, getting ready now!" I say.

"Patti? You're not wearing any makeup?"

I drop the phone stunned!

"Patti? Patti? Are you there?"

I am so angry with myself! What a silly error. Only Yolanda has seen me without my make up! I sigh, well it could have been worse, Marcus could have seen me without my makeup, wearing my do-rag and my glasses. Thankfully, I had at least put my contact lenses in!

I have been wearing prescription glasses since I was eight years old. It was bad enough being teased for being in foster care, but wearing national health specs in the 1970's meant I was mercilessly tormented at both primary and secondary school. So much so, I tried not to wear them, which meant I was always bumping into things and people. My studies suffered because I could not see the blackboard or see the print in my books. Veronica would send me off to school in the mornings wearing my glasses and I would take them off by the time I turned the corner to wait at the bus stop. I cannot count how many times my foster Mother took me to the opticians to replace my glasses. I got my tail cut after one parent's evening though, Veronica was holding them accountable for my poor grades and asked the teachers if I had been wearing my glasses to which the teachers all asked, "Does Patti wear glasses?"

The last guy who saw me wearing my glasses cruelly made a joke at my expense, so I remain sensitive about wearing them in public.

About two years ago, I attended the south region meeting of the Association of Black Probation Officers at head office in Victoria. One of the speakers was a man from an organisation called Clinks which is a social enterprise based in Brixton prison, who train prisoners in skills required to work in the restaurant business. Ian was encouraging the Association members to visit the restaurant within the prison and sample the menu. I expressed concerns about prisoners tampering with the food, but Ian assured that there was strict vetting of the prisoners involved in the programme and they worked alongside qualified chefs and other external staff. I made a mental note that I would arrange a trip for a few colleagues to visit the restaurant at HMP Brixton. After the meeting, Ian asked me out for a drink. I declined, as I do not drink alcohol. The reality is I should not drink alcohol, especially Southern Comfort.

The last time I drank Southern Comfort I got incredibly drunk very quickly. One minute I was stone cold sober dancing to Jah Cure's 'That Girl' and two drinks later, I was gyrating like a woman possessed to 'Gyal ah Bubble' by Konshens. I don't remember much else. I vomited in the minibus and the driver and my friends were not impressed at all. My friends said that once they got me indoors I stripped off all my clothes and walked up the stairs wearing only a thong. To this day I don't know how one of my high heels ended up in the en-suite loo. The following day I had to ring everyone to apologise and I made a pledge that Southern Comfort was not my friend and I would never drink alcohol again.

Ian did not let me get off the hook that easily, he asked me to join him for afternoon tea at Fortnum & Mason and I almost bit his hand off to say yes. I love afternoon teas in plush locations. I have had tea at Harrods, The Dorchester Hotel, The Hilton, and The Ritz several times and at Sandy Lane Hotel when I travelled to Barbados for my 40th birthday. Thank goodness, my Mum made it possible for me to see the beautiful Island where she grew up.

While I refreshed my make-up and splashed on some of my favourite perfume; Yellow Diamond by Versace after the meeting, Ian made the reservation for afternoon tea on his iPad and a few minutes later we were travelling on the tube to the restaurant in Piccadilly.

Ian turned out to be quite a funny guy. He was giving me nuff jokes about his experiences in working for Clinks; especially the amount of times he has been mistaken for an inmate, despite him wearing a suit and not prison issue sweats!

In no time at all, we arrived at the restaurant and we were escorted upstairs to take our seats in the Diamond Jubilee Celebration tearooms. I was taking in the opulent surroundings and furnishings. The tearoom was stunning with cream and gold walls with a grand piano. Our table was elegantly laid with pale blue and gold matching cups, saucers and side plates all made from fine bone china. I requested a glass of still water while I considered the menu. I could not quite see what I was reading so I dipped into my messenger bag for my reading glasses. Yes, I said to myself, I was going to forget I was trying to lose weight this week by eliminating bread from my diet. The finger sandwiches sounded delightful and I was determined to try the Fortnum's scones presented with Somerset cream and a choice of Fortnum & Mason preserves. Yes, I was going to enjoy everything on this menu. Now to figure out what type of tea I wanted. So, I took off my glasses and placed them on the table.

Ian was still in a jovial mood when he cheekily said, "Patti those glasses are so thick; I can see into the future!"

Then he laughed and laughed and laughed. I chuckled but I think he forgot where he was. People at the next tables began to stare at us and I felt incredibly self-conscious. Don't get me wrong I love to laugh but when the joke is on me it stops being funny and that was the last time, I wore my specs on a date. Fortnum & Mason ended up being one of my favourite places to visit but I never went out with Ian again. The man got too familiar with me too soon, for my liking…

…Oh my gosh, I forgot I was on a Skype call to Marcus!

"Patti, please pick up! I'm sorry Empress."

I pick up the phone and stare back at him. He smiles back at me. Oh, my days this man is FINE! He has just had his hair interlocked and styled by Morris Roots himself. I apologise for being silly and for scaring him. To which he tells me that I have beautiful skin and that I don't need to wear make-up at all. I blush and we make our final date night arrangements. I am meeting him at the Royal Albert Hall at 8 pm. Maya Blu is singing 'High Heels' from my iPod and I decide then and there I am going to put my high heels on for Marcus later tonight. I have been celibate for way too long. I am still a young woman and I have the need to feel beautiful tonight. I am excited as I select a brand new never worn matching red bra and knickers from Victoria's Secret to wear later and then I rush to get ready to meet up with Marcus.

5 ~ CHARMAINE

I beg my neighbour Marcia to look after the twins and let me borrow her car. She can see the words '**STRESSED OUT**' written across my forehead, so she consents after asking a few questions. She knows I would not ask unless I really needed to.

I quickly make my way to Thames Magistrates Court and park up in the virtually empty car park. I didn't even know that court buildings were even open on Saturday mornings. The security guard is friendly, even though I have interrupted him eating his cornflakes. He checks my handbag and ushers me through the security scanner. He tells me that all the overnight cases will be heard in courtroom one. I check the noticeboard outside the courtroom, and it confirms that Carlos Anthony Morgan is indeed appearing in court, but no details of the offence. The usher is of no use either. I sit at the back of the courtroom in the public gallery and wait. I take in my surroundings and the people in it.

The courtroom is like a stage, an old tired looking

stage, in need of a good lick of paint. Everybody looks like they are recovering from a hangover and moving in slow motion. I shudder to think what I must look like, as in my haste to get to court, I passed the flannel over myself in the 'sign of the cross', scrubbed my teeth and pulled on yesterday's clothes; my infamous black leggings and T-shirt. I don't think I stopped to cream my face or put on my deodorant. I quickly sniff under my armpit and I'm immediately repulsed by the smell. I seriously need to bathe when I get back home. I catch a glimpse of my reflection in the glass, which surrounds the public gallery, and although I avert my eyes quickly, it wasn't rapid enough. I see a fat haggard woman looking back at me. I must be a size 20 by now. How did that happen in four short years? My hairline is receding from continually dragging my hair back into a ponytail and my skin looks battered from not looking after myself properly. No wonder Junior strays, I am surprised he comes near me; I don't want to be near me.

I lean forward to try to catch what's being said but I can barely hear what's going on from where I am sitting. The woman from the CPS is outlining the prosecution case against an old Pakistani woman who stole from Primark. The old woman looks proper upset and full of shame. Primark? "Of all the places to steal from," I think with disdain. There are several designer shops up at Westfield to shoplift from, with quality gear. The stuff in 'Primarni' (as my Mum calls it) is bargain bucket and the clothes only last one season. I don't buy anything in there for the twins and when I lose some weight, I'm not shopping in there for myself either. Well, the Pakistani woman gets a fine for shoplifting and she is led outside by the duty solicitor.

Seizing my opportunity to find out what the hell has been going on; I follow them outside the courtroom. When he is done speaking to his client, I introduce myself as Charmaine Morgan, Junior's wife. He looks me up and down as if he's just trod in something and then he informs me that Junior got into a fight with a woman and broke her nose. When I ask who the woman was, he tells me to ask Junior for the details. I immediately go outside and light up a cigarette. I finish the cigarette in a couple of puffs, and I light another. Bloody bastard!

As I go back into the courtroom, Junior is sitting in the dock flanked by two SERCO security guards. He is slumped over, and his dreadlocks are covering his face. The CPS woman reads out the alleged offence. Now

41

hear this crock of shite; Junior went by this next woman's house and leaves at midnight. He suspects she has another man, so he sits in his car like he's flaming Colombo waiting to catch her out. Another geezer, a Mr Claremont (says the prosecution woman), shows up and is greeted passionately on the doorstep by the girl. An enraged Junior, jumps out of the car and beats up the pair of them, calling her a Slag and all sorts. A member of the public calls the police and it takes six police officers from City Road police station to tackle Junior. They beat his backside like Rodney King and cart his arse away from the scene.

All the time the CPS woman is addressing the court, Junior does not move a muscle. It's almost as though he knows I am there listening to all of this bullshit and watching his sorry arse. He stands up looks at me briefly, then as cool as a cucumber enters a guilty plea. His solicitor briefly addresses the court and the magistrate adjourns his case for three weeks for a Pre-Sentence Report; whatever that is. I wait an age for Junior to leave the cells and join me outside the courtroom. He speaks to his solicitor then some man from probation. Junior is advised to await a letter from the probation service for an interview with a probation officer. As we leave the court building, I try to speak to him, I need an explanation, but Junior is not in the mood to talk to me. I am practically running beside him as he makes giant strides to distance himself from me. I tell him I'm parked out the back; he curses and spins around almost bumping into me in his hurry to walk around the building to the car park. I am not about to be ignored, how bloody dare he? I open the car door and Junior jumps into the passenger seat. I sit beside him, but I don't start the engine.

I scream at him, "Junior just so I'm clear …you're having an affair with an outside woman and you catch the outside woman with her outside man, and you beat them both up? You fucking idiot!"

Before I could blink, Blam! Junior shot me a box right between my eyes. Blood instantly pours from my nose, which has already started to swell. I am dazed and too shocked to cry. I just stare back at him. Then I retaliate in true Charmaine style by head-butting him straight in the chin and then all hell breaks loose. We are punching, biting, scratching and cussing each other until our anger is spent. Without warning, I start the car and wheel spin out of the car park, travelling at speed, along Bow Road. Junior hits his head on the dashboard. I can tell my driving is scaring him and he's afraid, but he refuses to put his seatbelt on, and I carry on driving like I am Lewis Hamilton at Silverstone. I only slow down when I reach the one-way system at Stratford, as the last thing I want to do is hit a pedestrian in a car that I am not insured to drive, heck I don't even have a provisional licence!

Once we get indoors, I go straight upstairs to the bathroom and check my face out in the mirror. I suspect my nose is probably badly swollen, but not broken like Junior's outside woman's. I can see that the skin under my eyes is slowly turning an ugly shade of purple. I take off my stinky clothes and underwear. My breasts are saggy, and my stomach resembles a road map caused by stretch marks. My whole face stings as I climb into the shower and the warm water hits my face. The tears start to flow uncontrollably right there under the hot jet of the water. My arms ache from fighting and I see new bruises merging with the old ones. I sob even harder. What have I done to deserve this? How could Junior cheat on me again? I have had enough of this, I need to get out of this marriage, but I don't know how!

A whole hour passes before I emerge from the bathroom. Junior is asleep in my unmade bed, with his stinky self and two black eyes. I dress, comb my hair back into a ponytail and strategically apply some foundation to my face. I compose myself and I go next door to Marcia's. She gasps when she sees my face, but she does not comment. I stay there for the rest of the day.

6 ~ ROSE

Be careful what you ask God for; I prayed that Manley would not be able to accompany me to the doctor's surgery for my six-week check. I got my wish, but the circumstances are heartbreaking. Manley was on the internet the entire night looking for cheap flights to Jamaica. We decided my Mum would take care of the girls whilst we're away, but that the baby will be travelling with us. I left Manley sorting out the passports for me and Esther as my passport had run out a while back, but we could not yet afford to get it renewed. I was also not aware that Esther would need to have her own passport. How ridiculous was that?

Esther's complexion and features had already changed significantly since she had been born six weeks ago. She was very pale almost white when she was born, but I could tell by the colouring around her ears she was going to darken to a shade similar to her father's. In fact, all the girls were dark-skinned like their Dad. She will look nothing like her passport photo in 12 months' time, but if baby needs a passport Manley will just have to pay for it. The 'love' offering collected from the congregation yesterday will more than cover the costs. Manley spoke to Junior last night, but he could not get hold of Marcus, so reluctantly he left several messages for him to contact him urgently. I know I should not have favourites, but I really get on with Marcus. He is really hands-on with the girls, taking them out and spending quality time with them. Junior, on the other hand, is a different kettle of fish. Back in the day Junior had a hit with a reggae song and was a minor celebrity, but he has not been able to produce a hit since the 90s and because of his lifestyle, otherwise known as weed smoking, we do not see him, Charmaine or the twins very often. Junior, as my gran (God rest her soul), would say, "is pretty from afar, but far from pretty". The brothers will be taking time off work to attend their dad's funeral. We will meet them in Jamaica and stay together at the family home in Negril, Westmoreland, as there is ample room for us all there.

I make a mental note to ask Dr Oko what immunisation Esther needs to have before we travel. I am feeling sad with the turn of events in the last 24 hours. Pops Morgan never got to hold Esther, but thanks be to God and the wonders of face time Pops got to see her a few hours after she was born.

I am sitting in the dingy waiting room watching the LED, which will eventually display my name, and I read the information on the screen like I have never seen it before. I am hoping the doctor mentions contraception so I can find out what it is all about. I have not been able to look up anything on the internet as I have had my hands full with the arrival of my baby. I heard on the news about a new contraceptive injection and I want to know more about it. Manley believes that it is the will of the Lord when and if we will have another child, but to be fair it's not Manley who's carried FIVE babies in the last 10 years and it was definitely not Manley who'd had a caesarean six weeks ago which was almost fatal. I see my name on the screen and I gingerly navigate the pram down a series of doors and corridors to room 8. Doctor Oko my Nigerian doctor warmly greets me as an old friend. She is also a pastor's wife. We have visited their church and they have visited ours.

Dr Oko starts with Esther first by weighing her. Thankfully, Esther has regained the weight she lost about two weeks ago and is doing well. I am examined next and she is impressed with how the scar from the caesarean is healing. There was a time at the end when I thought that would never recover from the procedure.

I attended hospital with my Mum six weeks ago for a routine antenatal appointment. When the midwife Effie took my blood pressure, it was sky high. She was so concerned I had to wait to see the registrar. I was quite cool about things because I had high blood pressure for short periods throughout my pregnancy and I was now in the last trimester. When I eventually saw the consultant, he helped me to lie down on the bed. He was a lovely chap from Egypt, and he went through my medical notes with me before examining me. He jokingly asked if I was having twins as he could feel two heads. Then he delivered the bad news. I needed to have an emergency caesarean that day as my blood pressure was too high and I was at risk of having a stroke. Sometimes we say some silly things when we're in shock. I told the doctor in no uncertain terms that I could not have my baby today because I had not yet packed my hospital bag. Furthermore, after this appointment, my Mother and I had plans to go to Mothercare World in Edmonton off the A406 to do some shopping. It was my Mum who convinced me to listen to the professionals and that she would call Manley to tell him to get to the hospital. My Mum quickly prayed with me and left the room to make some calls to arrange for a church sister to sit with the girls. Sensing the panic rising by the minute in my voice, my midwife Effie who had delivered my other babies, explained that although she was about to go off duty, she would stay with me until my baby was born.

Things happened pretty quickly after the decision was made. I undressed and wore an undignified white hospital gown with the back open to for the entire world to see and I was given a blue hairnet and white surgical stockings to wear. Effie inserted a catheter into my left hand, and I was weighed again. My Mum had not yet been able to contact Manley, who was probably out pricing up a job. A German doctor introduced herself to me as the anaesthetist who would be administering the epidural. When I saw the breed of needle she was going to insert into my spine I started to pray and cry. It was more crying than praying if I'm honest, but I am confident that God understood my tears. Effie held my hands and encouraged me to curve my spine. The doctor tried twice to insert the needle, but I kept on shaking. I could not help it. I think it was a combination of nerves and feeling cold. The doctor gave me a stern talking to, saying she was going to try to insert the needle in my back one last time and if it did not work after that, I would have to have a general anaesthetic. I reasoned with myself; if I went down that route, I would not see my baby for some time after its birth, so I held onto Effie's hands, gritted my teeth and trusted the doctor with my life. Still no Manley, but at least when my Mum came back in the room she reported that she had got hold of him and he was on his way. The next thing I recall I was on the gurney being transported by a porter to theatre. We were all holding on for Manley to be present. The staff busied themselves with their monitors and equipment. I was now attached to monitors on my chest and could hear my own heart beating reassuringly from a machine nearby. All the time I was praying silently, willing the Lord to send Manley in.

"So, tell me Mrs Morgan do you have other children?" Inquired the Egyptian doctor.

He was dressed in blue scrubs and wearing a facemask, but I recognised his voice.

I must have mentioned the four girls to which he replied, "Well we're hoping for a boy today."

All I remember next was the heart monitor slowing down. I blacked out momentarily. I had an oxygen mask put on my face and the doctor was yelling to get my

Mother in a gown and get her in here. I was not in a position to protest. The next person by my side was Manley. He was wearing blue scrubs and a facial mask like the other staff. I knew he was smiling behind the mask and my stats instantly improved.

"Sorry my darling, I got stuck in traffic, but I wouldn't miss this for the world, I love you Rose".

Then the weirdest thing happened next as they started the operation. As they were cutting away to get to my womb, I left my body and started to float up and almost hover above the bed with my back against the ceiling. I was not scared, and I was not in pain. I had a bird's eye view of everything. I could see everyone panicking to revive me and Manley praying with a Ladbroke's betting slip hanging out of his back pocket. I saw when they reached my womb and burst my waters, I saw them wiggling the baby out and I saw that the baby was a girl all pink and covered in blood. "Well, at least I have seen my baby girl before I die." I thought sadly. However, God had other plans because I drifted slowly back into my body to be told officially that my baby girl was here. I turned to look at her and she was beautiful. A rush of hormones instantly flooded my body and I began to cry tears of joy. I watched Manley cut the cord and kiss our baby on the forehead, he could not have looked any happier. Effie swiftly took the baby from him and out of the corner of my eye; I could see they were using an instrument to clear her lungs. I was aware that they were going to give her vitamin K injection to aide her blood clotting and when they pricked her heel, she started to cry.

After I'd had a blood transfusion, we were conveyed to the maternity ward and assisted by the staff there to get settled in. After greeting her latest granddaughter my Mum left to return later with all the things I would need and some much-needed nourishment. Surprisingly, I felt really good but then I realised it was because the anaesthetic had not yet worn off. I went straight into nurturing mode eager for baby to latch onto my breast. Manley looked on proudly, adjusting my pillows and making sure, I was in a comfortable position. Esther latched on straightaway but experience taught me that there would be a delay in my milk arriving as she was seven weeks early and classified as a premature baby. But we gave God thanks because we both made it through by His grace and Esther did not require any further medical intervention. My 5lbs and 11 ounces of deliciousness was alive, well and hungry!

"Rosie! I am so proud of you!" said Manley kissing me gently on the lips. "Thank you my darling, thank you." He continued.

"Are you disappointed she's not a boy?" I asked.

"No, not really babes every baby is a gift from God, and I'm blessed," he replied.

"So how much did you lose?" I asked.

"Lose? What do you mean Rosie?" He inquired.

"Betting Manley, I saw the slip in your back pocket!" I exclaimed.

Now, at my post birth six week appointment, Dr Oko completed her examination of me, and typed up her notes whilst I got dressed. Thankfully, my blood pressure had returned to normal and other than sore nipples from nursing Esther I was in good physical shape. I had gained half a stone in weight, which I was confident I would lose, once I resumed the school runs and my other errands.

"Mrs Morgan, please tell me, how are you feeling within yourself?"

Whilst I was expecting the question, I was not expecting my reaction to her questioning and I burst into tears. Dr Oko offered me a tissue and waited for me to compose myself. I told her that my father in law had passed away last night and we were due to travel to Jamaica the following week. Dr Oko appeared to understand but nonetheless took me through a series of questions from her screen to assess whether I was suffering from postnatal depression. She was keen to see me again once I returned from the funeral. We spoke about contraception and I said I wanted more information regarding the side effects before making my final decision, but I was eager to start something before travelling. My doctor recommended the mini pill and she printed a four-week prescription, which would cover my time away in Jamaica. When I went to apologise for my outburst she told me to behave myself and wished us all the best. I took the prescription to be dispensed at the chemist next door to the surgery. I stood up right there in the shop and took my first tablet with a bottle of Evian water. I discarded the box and placed the strip of tablets in my purse.

All the knowledge of what you do in secret comes out in the light…eventually.

7 ~ PATTI

Years ago when I was studying for my Masters a guy from my Action Learning Set took me on a date to watch an opera at the Royal Albert Hall. It was Madame Butterfly. The experience was breathtaking. So, when Marcus suggested that we go to see the ballet I was very impressed. In my experience, it is very rare for black men to be interested in ballet, but Marcus is so different from all the other men I have dated.

Whilst waiting for the show to start, Marcus talks about the ballet lessons he had as a child when he first arrived in the country. He said he could still remember some of the feet positions and he would show me a couple of moves later! I blushed and fanned myself with my fan and we both laughed. I asked him why he stopped dancing and he explained that by the time he reached secondary school he had discovered Hip Hop and never looked back.

We made plans to see the 'Straight Outta Compton'

film when it was released in September. I was happy to be part of his future plans and suggested that he stayed at mine tonight. His eyes lit up when I explained Yolanda would be away for the night. Well 'Mister Man' held my hand throughout the first act of the ballet leaving only momentarily during the interval and returning with a glass of red wine for him and a soft drink for me.

As I had never seen the ballet before, Marcus was able to break down the story of Swan Lake for me so I could understand. I have to admit that every time he whispered in my ear; I was being turned on so much, that I had to cross my legs. As the second act started, I was thinking how events would turn out later. I had not been in an intimate situation for nearly two years. What if I'd forgotten what to do?

After the ballet, Marcus and I travel back to Ilford station to pick up his car and he drives a short distance to a new Caribbean Restaurant called Ginger Sky. I have ordered takeaways from there in the past but have never eaten in. I'm impressed with the décor and the warm welcome given by the staff. As we walk to our table I spot Martin, affectionately known as 'Shoe doctor' eating in the corner with some of his DJ mates. He rises to greet me with kisses on both cheeks and then he and Marcus greet each other like long-lost brethren. From what I can gather over the noise of the busy restaurant, Marcus and Martin go back years. Apparently, they attended the same college back in the day. What a small world? The lads exchange mobile telephone numbers and Martin gives Marcus a couple of flyers for an event he has coming up. Martin tells him to bring me, 'his missus' down to Bojangles nightclub in Chingford as well.

I beam back at Marcus and he is grinning like the cat that's got the cream. I'm too nervous to eat but I manage a small portion of ackee and saltfish, preferring to sip on my glass of soursop punch. Marcus eats a large portion of curry goat and rice plus the remainder of my meal, stating that he needs to build up his strength. I almost spit out my drink, he really knows how to make me laugh. I let him know that he needs to be gentle with me because it's been quite some time. He reassures me that everything is going to be fine.

Once we arrive back at my home, I make Marcus a drink and tell him to give me a few minutes before joining me upstairs in my bedroom. Thankfully, my bed is made with clean sheets and my room is immaculate. I freshen up in the en-suite, brushing my teeth rigorously as I had eaten fish. I put on my red underwear and red high heels, wink at my gorgeous self in the mirror and lie on my king size bed waiting for Marcus to come upstairs and join me, 'Cheese on Bread' as my Mum would say…

I cannot quite believe Marcus is dancing at the foot of my bed in nothing more than his underwear and he's really good at this ballet thing for real, I'm impressed. I applaud at the end of my private ballet performance and I ask him if he's ready for me to which he replies, "Mi born ready Empress."

Mum was eager to pass on all her pearls of wisdom to me as soon as I could talk and when it came to talking about 'the facts of life', she had a frank candid discussion with me about it. The conversation ending with, "Your private life should be just that; PRIVATE and your bedroom business is precisely that too, your bedroom business!"

With those nuggets in mind, I would love to tell you chapter and verse about what went down between Marcus and I, but I am going to have to keep that between him and me. What I will share though, is the fact that I was not at all disappointed and that size truly does matter.

I wake from my sleep and turn over to gaze at the sleeping man in my bed who is solely responsible for my happiness right now. I kiss him briefly on the lips and I exit the bed to use the bathroom. After that, I tug on my fluffy dressing gown, slip my mobile phone into my pocket and quietly tiptoe downstairs. I check my messages and there is a WhatsApp from Yolanda, confirming that she went out raving and is now back at Jo-Anne's house.

Now, what shall I make Marcus for breakfast? I have all the ingredients for a really good fry up, but something tells me Marcus does not eat pork, so I make coffee and two hot bowls of cornmeal porridge, just like Mum taught me. When I get back to the bedroom, Marcus is awake sitting up in my bed looking sexy as hell.

"Good Morning Beautiful, and how are we doing today?" He enquires.

"Feeling on top of the world, thanks to you," I reply as I place the tray on the bed, "How are you feeling?" I ask passing him a bowl and spoon,

"Well after I finish this, why don't I show you?"

I nearly spit out my herbal tea with laughter. So, this is how the rest of our morning pans out, a pattern of lovemaking and eating, taking it in turns to venture downstairs to scavenge for much-needed sustenance. Marcus must have found his way around my kitchen because he comes back upstairs with a batch of fried dumplings and they taste delicious! Later we dine on a yummy fruit salad, beautifully handcrafted by Marcus and I am confident that my fridge is now empty and that I will have to do a shop tomorrow. For now, we are entwined under the duvet covers deciding what to watch on TV. Marcus flicks through the channels using the remote and we settle down to watch X Factor on ITV 2. We already know the outcome of the show and we watch it again convinced that Anton Stephens was robbed of his place by one of the judges who called him 'fake' on live TV the night before.

Marcus switches on his mobile phone, it slowly flickers into life and what follows is a series of alerts indicating missed calls, text messages, and the phone lights up like a Christmas Tree. Marcus is so alarmed by this he is suddenly sitting bolt upright in bed. Seeing the look of panic on his face makes me panic too!

"What's wrong, Marcus what's wrong!" I scream.

"It's Manley, my big Brother; he's been trying to get hold of me all day. Patti, it's my father…he's dead."

8 ~ CHARMAINE

I have not been speaking To Junior for three weeks, other than to ask him when he's going to leave. The way Junior reacts, anyone would think I was the one who cheated on him! I have nothing further to say to him. In the interim period, Junior is acting like father of the flaming year; taking care of the twins, taking them to nursery, cooking and cleaning and even reading them a bedtime story.

He even comes to the first session of the triple P Programme (It stands for Positive Parenting Programme) we were referred to by the nursery, because of the change in the twins' behaviour. Whilst Junior and I thought the children were playing with their toys they were in fact, listening to our adult conversations; my little satellite dishes! Some of the conversations were not pleasant and we always seemed to be fighting in front of them.

This impacted on my confidence and my ability to discipline them. They only listened to my Mum and they swore constantly. On more than one occasion, the children have embarrassed me by swearing on the bus or in the supermarket. It was only a matter of time before they got me in hot water with social services. I was trying to see everything as a positive rather than a negative as I was ready to make changes in my life and in the life of my children.

The first session was about setting boundaries, and having, and sticking to a routine. I figured with Junior going to prison I would need to take back authority as a parent and get back control of my children.

The kids' key worker Aronda was a lovely black woman a little bit older than me with a warm smile and at least 200 curly sisterlocs cascading down her back. She'd coloured some of them blonde, which complimented her complexion. 'Dumb and Dumber' ran to her as usual for a cuddle before going to the outside area to ride on one of the tricycles and play on the slides. Aronda usually always wore jeans with the nursery logo T-shirts and an apron, either preparing for an activity with the children or clearing away after an activity, but today she was in training mode and dressed in a trouser suit with a white shirt with a navy blazer.

We were escorted through the nursery to the meeting room at the back of the building. The other advantage about being on the course was that the twins could stay at the nursery all day and all their meals would be provided. No cooking later on for me I thought. I'll have a tuna salad when I get back from my run in the park. Junior would have to sort himself out. Junior had taken to cooking up a storm in the kitchen and the children were loving it. They could even manage the heat from his pepper soup but by far, they loved his fried dumplings the most. I devoured one when I thought he wasn't looking, and I did an extra lap around the park to make up for cheating on my diet. In my mind, Junior cooking and attending this class was all for show and I wasn't going to fall for it.

The meeting room was really nice. Smaller tables were put together to make a larger one with chairs on the outskirts. I sat as near as I could to the windows where I could observe the children playing outside. It was a warm day for September and the staff wore cardigans over their T-shirts.

Aronda had forewarned us that there would be parents attending the programme who were referred by the family courts and faced the removal of their children. Some parents had volunteered as they wanted to brush up on their parenting skills and some had been referred by the nursery, like us. The room filled up quickly. There were twelve of us in total. The majority were single parents and another couple besides Junior and me. Aronda started the day with what she called an ice-breaker.

"Introduce yourself to the group by your first name and say one thing you're hoping to learn from the programme today."

Flipping over the flipchart paper, she held out the pen and asked me to write up everybody's answer, as I was the closest. I was mortified and could have died on the spot. Seeing she was not going to budge, I reluctantly got up from my seat and joined her upfront. Aronda encouraged me by saying not to worry about my handwriting or spelling all the sheets were for the eyes of this group only. I took the flipchart pen as Aronda went around the room. She occasionally turned around to make eye contact with me and to ensure I was keeping up with what was being said. I was reassured by this and got into my stride. After the exercise, we had generated two pages worth of notes, which Aronda said we would revisit at the end of the course.

When I sat back down Junior said, "Well done Charms, you looked like a natural up there."

I brushed off the compliment but inwardly I was

chuffed. I wondered where I would be in life if I had applied myself at school. I wasn't a dummy I knew that much. Up until year 9, I was an A* student. After my Dad died, I gave up. He wasn't in my corner anymore.

My Mum lost the plot overwhelmed with grief. She rarely came out; she stopped talking to me, as though I was somehow responsible for my Dad's death. She stopped opening letters and paying bills. She didn't let me in so we could grieve together. She took so much time off work at Lesneys toy factory in Hackney that she missed out on the opportunity to move to Peterborough when the factory closed down.

She went through the motions of being a parent to me and I felt so isolated and alone. I'd spend hours in my room listening to music when I stumbled across a pirate station playing dancehall music. I easily found like-minded girls at school to hang around with and we bunked off school to watch the music channels and learn the latest dance moves. If I had studied my books like I studied those dance moves I'd be a fucking rocket scientist by now. I kissed my teeth. Junior thought I was kissing my teeth at him, but I couldn't be bothered to explain myself.

What was really useful was the session after lunch.

Junior and I designed a schedule with the pens and crayons given to us. Junior was good at the layout and agreeing the tasks we needed to complete. For example, the children would wake at 7:30 am and must be in bed by 7 pm. We jointly agreed who would wash them in the mornings whilst the other parent got breakfast ready. We agreed who would bath them at night and who would read them a story at bedtime. We even agreed what meals they would eat during the week, which would make shopping and budgeting easy. Aronda explained to all the parents that it would be tough in the beginning but ultimately children loved and needed routine.

I blurted out, "I figure I could roll with anything if it meant those brats were asleep from 7 pm until 7 am. Twelve hours of bliss."

The other parents laughed but Aronda did not find my comments funny at all. Instead, she focused on insisting that we called our children by their proper names. Name-calling even subconsciously, negatively affects the way we interact with our children. Her comments were a bit 'arty farty' to me but we wanted our children to change and that meant we had to change too. I apologised and made a vow to myself to do better.

At the end of the first session we swapped numbers

with a couple of the women to offer each other moral support, Junior carefully rolled up our schedule, and we went to collect the twins. They both rushed to us.

"Mummy, Daddy!" They squealed pleased to see us both at nursery together.

"Hey, Gaby and Gary!" We said in unison and Junior scooped them both up.

"Let's go and put your coats on... where's your peg?" he asked.

"But we don't want to put our coats on!" cried Gaby.

"Gaby, you need to do as your Daddy says," I said backing him up.

"Ok," said Gaby backing down "I'll show you where my peg is Daddy."

"And I'll show you where my peg is, Mummy," Gary said excitedly.

Junior turned to me and winked "One module at a time Charms."

To me, this change in behaviour signals how worried he is about the outcome of the court case. I was led to believe he was due to go back to Thames Magistrates Court but when I read the letter from his solicitor which Junior had discarded on the table, I became aware that he was going up the road to Snaresbrook Crown Court and facing at least two years in prison. "Good!" I thought, two years of bliss, two years of happiness, and two years of knowing exactly where he is.

Junior had seen his solicitor alone a couple of times in East Ham, but when he asks me to attend an appointment with the probation service with him I simply answer, "Yes."

On the day of the appointment, Junior is smartly dressed, dreadlocks tied back, and he has all of his documentation together in a folder to show the people dem from probation. We leave the twins next door with Marcia and catch the bus to Stratford. I know exactly where the probation building is on Romford Road as I have passed it several times on the bus to Ilford. I never imagined that I would be going inside the building though. We are buzzed in and walk up the stairs to the first floor. The first thing that hits you is how stinky the waiting room is. 'Shit! Someone needs to open all the windows in here,' I think to myself, 'seriously!'

Junior tells the receptionist his name and shows her his appointment letter. We are advised to take a seat and wait. At 10 am in the morning, the waiting area is already filled with punters. They are mainly men and mainly black men, which I find quite concerning. Junior because of his stupidity is now one of them, a service user.

To my relief, a smartly dressed black man calls Junior's name and he introduces himself as the probation officer who will be interviewing him today. I rise to go in, but the officer tells me I am not permitted to join them. He is polite when speaking to me but to the point. To be honest, I do not want to be present; which wife in her right mind wants to hear the intimate details of her husband's affair? I am happy to leave them all to it.

I descend the stairs rapidly escaping from the stench of the waiting room into the fresh air. I walk up to Stratford Shopping Mall, walking through the grounds of St John's Parish Church where Junior and I got hitched. From the looks of things, it is warming up to be a lovely day. I take my tracksuit top off and tie it around my waist. I believe I have a couple of hours to myself and I pick up the pace to get to Westfield Shopping Centre. I have really found the last few weeks stressful and the tension between Junior and me is at times overwhelming. But this time I don't resort to eating everything in sight. I feel lighter even though I have not plucked up the courage to step on the bathroom scales. I've taken to walking around the West Ham Park every day and I attempted to jog yesterday. You would be surprised how many people are over there first thing in the morning or an hour before it closes either running, walking or jogging. Junior probably wonders where I disappear to, but I do not have to answer to him, all he needs to know is I am not having an affair! Thank goodness, Primark is virtually empty.

I head for the women's department and try to remember the last time I bought something nice for myself other than a pair of black leggings. I will know what I am looking for when I see it and when I do, I go for my usual size, which is a size 20. When I hand my items to the cashier, she suggests I try them on in the changing rooms first. I reluctantly head to the changing rooms and try the outfit on. To my complete shock and delight, the suit is too big for me. The same cashier winks at me when I re-present at the till with my size 16 dress suit.

By the time I get back to the Probation Office, Junior is outside smoking a cigarette. He tells me the interview went well, but there is a chance he will go to prison, because of the injuries the victim suffered. For fear of getting into another fight, I say nothing, but the words 'Serve your ass right' are on the edge of my spiteful bitter tongue. Junior observes my bag containing my new purchases, but he knows he cannot ask me anything about it. When he's finished smoking, we walk back to the bus stop.

On the day of the court case, I am up early for my morning walk, then I get the twins ready for nursery. My Mum will take them to nursery in the afternoon. Junior looks very dapper in his new suit and dress shoes. He has also packed a bag with the essential items he thinks he will need for prison. I have a shower and paint my fingernails on the edge of the bathroom sink. I apply my foundation and new red lipstick. Instead of my usual ponytail, I arrange my hair into a high bun. I wear my faux pearl earrings and choker, which my Mother gave me for my birthday years ago. I was hoping to wear them for a special occasion and then I realise today is a special occasion; Junior is being sent down, he is finally getting what he deserves.

When I finally join Junior downstairs in the living room, I can tell he's impressed. Funny thing is three weeks ago, I would have loved for him to be looking at me the way he is now, but today I do not care!

"Wow Charms!" exclaims my Mum, "You look fantastic! Mind you don't meet a young barrister down there!" Mum teases.

Junior is obviously upset by her comment, "Come on

Charmaine, the cab's outside."

The journey from Pelly Road to Snaresbrook Crown Court is completed in silence, even the cab driver knew not to make any noise or strike up a conversation. Wanstead is not that far away from Plaistow but the difference in the houses and green spaces is remarkable. I can't help but feel resentful because we could have been living in one of those big houses with a big garden if it wasn't for Junior and his wastefulness.

At the height of his singing success, he let a lot of big money fall through his hands because he was living large instead of saving his money. I just about managed to hold on to some money to buy our little ex-council house, but it's too small for us now and the children will soon need their own bedrooms. Junior had just the one hit, a couple of nice suits and a pair of designer shoes to show for it. I can't remember the last time Junior said he was going to the studio and even if he did I wouldn't believe him anyway.

The cab turns right into the grounds of the court and stops outside the entrance to the lobby. The building is intimidating and awesome, so much different from Thames Magistrates Court. For the first time, I feel scared, even though I haven't done anything wrong.

Once inside the court building, we pass through security and I see Marcus looking out for us on the other side. He greets me and Junior warmly and we make our way to courtroom number 5.

Marcus looks fit and as yummy as I remember. He is wearing a black suit with a crisp white shirt and black tie we make small talk about the twins as we walk to the courtroom. I am so glad that despite their quarrels Marcus is here for his brother. As we reach to courtroom Junior greets the duty solicitor, who in turn introduces him to his brief, a mature black woman; I instantly dislike her and it is obvious she thinks she's all that and a bag of chips, in her black gown and 'poxy' wig. In fact, most people are prancing up and down looking extremely busy, walking about like their shit don't stink. Junior's solicitor looks at me and smiles approvingly at me like I passed the 'loyal wife test.' I kiss my teeth and turn my head in the opposite direction. I take a book out of my handbag as I hear Junior attempting to ridicule me for reading a book. He asks me what I am reading so I show him the title and he stops his banter immediately.

"I don't know why you've started reading all them books for Charms, those feminist bitches don't even like men, they wanna break up families!"

As calmly as I can, I say back to him, "Junior no feminist forced you to cheat on your wife and then beat up your girlfriend."

"Why have you got to keep bringing that up for?" He snorts, "That happened ages ago."

I don't bother to reply.

The barrister then calls Junior into a side room to read the Pre-Sentence Report, which the man from probation wrote.

"Charmaine don't listen to Junior he's stressed out about the case. I think there's nothing sassier than a woman trying to educate herself," says Marcus.

He then winks at me and I smile and return to reading my book. However, I'm not reading my book at all; I am thinking about Marcus and how warm and fuzzy he makes me feel whenever I see him. All I can think is, 'I went and married the wrong brother.'

When Junior returns he mentions the barrister will be pushing for the judge to follow the recommendation in the report, which is a community payback order and a requirement to complete a domestic abuse programme.

I continue to read my book unimpressed by what he has said. It's almost 3 pm when Junior's case is called. I sit in the public gallery with Marcus facing the judge. The barrister from the CPS is going through the summary again and then Junior's barrister addresses the court putting forward mitigating circumstances including the fact that Junior's father has recently passed away. This is the first time I am hearing this! What! I look at Marcus who looks pained, but I am still confused. I want to stand up and address the court and tell them that Junior is lying, but then just one look at Junior's contorted face confirms that his dad has died... ...Why didn't the little bitch tell me? I know we haven't been exactly on speaking terms, but that kinda shit I need to hear directly from him, not from his 'poxy' barrister at court. I look at Marcus quizzically, he says that he thought I knew, but he didn't think Junior would try to use their father's death to get a lighter sentence, how shameful; their dad would be so ashamed to see one of his children in court. As he spoke, I started to wonder what else was written in that Pre-Sentencing Report that I knew nothing about. What did he say about me during his interview?

The Court rose to consider sentence and Junior rushed outside to chain smoke. He was visibly upset and anxious about losing his liberty.

"Junior, I'm very sorry to hear about Pops," I said with all the sympathy I could muster. "You know you should have told me."

Junior looked at me and replied, "I didn't know how to, with all that's been going on Charms. I'm sorry, really sorry about everything. If I get off today, I want to go home to bury my father. My Mum needs me, and I want you to come too."

"Ok Junior, let's just see what happens." I take my seat back in the public gallery and listen quietly as the judge says he's going to follow the recommendation outlined in the Pre-Sentence Report. I sit back in my seat and I curse the judge, the probation officer and the flash barrister under my breath. You people are sending this fucking madman back into my home. I catch Marcus looking at me and I break into a huge fake smile.

9 ~ ROSE

The last week has absolutely flown by and I cannot quite believe we are sitting on a British Airways flight to Kingston. My Mum and my church prayer group came over to help me pack and prayed with my family. When the prayer meeting finished I put the girls to bed and said goodbye. We planned to leave home for 6 am and decided that I would not wake them up at that hour. I had a lump in my throat as I closed their bedroom door. This was the first time that I would be leaving them for so long, but they were going to be in good hands. I brought down a spare duvet and a pillow for my Mum and helped her to get comfortable on the sofa. From tomorrow night, my Dad would be sleeping over too but they would be sleeping in our bed.

I was woken at about 2 am by Esther crying for her feed. She latched on like she, had not eaten all day and I winced with the pain. Manley slept soundly next to me.

After she'd had her fill, I changed her nappy and put her back in her Moses basket and I switched off the bedside lamp. I was awoken again, this time by Manley. Apparently, he was hungry too. I protested saying I was tired and still sore from the caesarean, but he would not listen. He was not loving towards me at all, no kisses or cuddles, which I would have preferred. There were no terms of endearment, no affection whatsoever. Not even an attempt at foreplay or intimacy at all, just a quickie for him to release some tension. I felt hurt, violated, used and empty. In a matter of minutes, Manley was back asleep. I could not sleep so I got up and tip toed to the bathroom to have a hot shower. I prayed that enough of the contraception was in my system to avoid another pregnancy.

I spend the next few hours on the landing where I set up the ironing board and press the children's school uniforms and Sunday school clothes. I love ironing:- the whole process of creating steam and turning material which is all crumpled up into beautiful pleats on Pinfold dresses and skirts and crisp clean seams down Manley's suit trousers. This chore was made easier by the steam iron I begged Manley to buy for me from the TV shopping channel. The investment did not disappoint.

All I have to do is plug the iron in, make sure the base is filled to the correct level and leave it a couple of minutes to heat up the water. I'd soon have instant steam to power through at least a basket full of clothes, After I tackle the clothes, I iron the bedsheets and pillowcases, leaving the towels until last. I praise myself for a job well done but all the while I am thinking of what happened in my bedroom and what lies in store for me in Jamaica. I try to be positive by focusing on seeing my Uncle and Mother Morgan again, as I silently pack away the ironing into the girl's wardrobes. I kiss each daughter on the forehead before closing their bedroom door behind me and place the towels in the linen cupboard and go back to lie down for a couple of hours.

Two hours later, we are checking in at Gatwick airport. The cabin crew look after us well; especially when they find out, we are attending a funeral in Jamaica. Esther is the star of the show; she hardly reacts to the plane taking off, much to the delight of the other passengers. Esther coos in all the right places and we have a request from a special passenger travelling in first class to see our baby. I am delighted to present our baby to none other than Portia Simpson-Miller the Prime Minister of Jamaica! I am thrilled to take Esther to first class to meet her. I am grinning away like the Queen Mum. For a moment, my mood shifts, and I feel lighter, the feeling of despair only returns when I sit back in economy next to Manley. The only break I have from the baby during the flight is when I go to use the loo. I don't get to see any of the in-flight entertainment because I am either feeding or changing Esther, with no help from Manley. Thankfully, a member of the cabin crew is besotted with Esther and takes her for a half an hour so I can eat my meal.

I cannot speak for anyone else but the older I get, the longer the journey feels. The 10 hours from London Gatwick to Jamaica feels more like 20 hours. I do not have any ambition to travel to Australia, but only God knows how people manage that kind of journey; it would finish me off! I am fighting the urge to scream, "Are we there yet?" when the pilot announces that we will be making our descent into Kingston Norman Manley International Airport. The island looks as beautiful as I remember when we came to Jamaica the first Christmas after Manley's parents returned.

As soon as the plane door opens, a rush of warm air consumes the aircraft and we all begin to sweat. Esther begins to scream, and tourists are rushing to get off the plane to start their package holidays. I give thanks that we have arrived safely, and I take a layer of clothing off Esther in an attempt to keep her cool and comfortable. I successfully manage to get Esther downstairs and follow Manley into the newly renovated airport. Although we are in Jamaica for a sad occasion, I am happy to be home once more.

The newly upgraded airport looks so impressive and I can tell the tourists are impressed too. I burst with pride as we twist and turn down to the arrivals hall to retrieve our luggage. I am so proud to be a Jamaican right now. We have a brand new international airport with all the mod cons just like JFK and Gatwick airports. The airport staff are smartly dressed in their uniforms and everything is running efficiently. I am pleasantly surprised to see staff sporting their natural hair and some of the men and women have locked their hair in the most amazingly creative styles. If I was not the Pastor's wife I would have locked up my hair a long time ago like Rita Marley.

Anyway, Manley quickly appraises and recruits one of the red cap porters to look out for our luggage whilst I sit down with Esther. I am comforted by the sweet Jamaican accents, the jesting and banter of the red cap men and the taxi drivers and soon we're outside the airport enjoying the warm evening sunshine waiting for our driver to bring the car around.

When I get into the car with Esther I am hit by the driver's really bad BO. It is so bad I feel nauseous, so I lift up my face towards the sun, close my eyes and feel the rays warm up my face. The heat from the sun feels wonderful. I crack open the window in an attempt to get some fresh air and to soak in as much vitamin D as I can before the sun sets.

I was born and bred in Jamaica, yet I am struggling to understand what the driver Lennox and Manley are chattering about as we make our way to Long Bay. Esther is asleep and whilst I am tired too I gaze out of the window to take in all the scenery while there is still daylight. We travel down the highway west of the airport passing many hotels along the way and I wonder what kind of holiday the tourists on the plane are going to have trapped in an all-inclusive hotel. We are two hours into our three-hour journey, driving south-west, passing through the parish of Westmoreland. Everything is so green and vibrant in comparison to grey old London Town, so bright that it hurts my eyes. Our driver drives the car like he stole it and the police are chasing him, so much so that I have to balance Esther in one hand and hold on with the other. The people look so colourful too, dressed in sunshine colours going about their daily lives. I can hear reggae music everywhere competing with an orchestra of crickets and toads. I put on my sunglasses and I take it all in. All I need now is a glass of fresh coconut water and I will have arrived in paradise.

We pull up outside Manley's parent's home in pitch darkness. Young men who I don't know appear out of the darkness and assist in taking our luggage out of the car. Manley pays Lennox and the men, and we walk up a couple of steps on to the veranda into the house. Mother Morgan elegantly comes to greet us. She has lost a lot of weight and it suits her, her smile is still warm and inviting. She hugs me so tightly I think she's going to suffocate poor Esther who begins to cry but stops when she sees her gran.

"Bless the Lord...yuh reach!"

I wish I had volunteered to pray because it would have been short and sweet. Manley had an audience, so he had to pray for everybody in the village and to bless and thank everyone. He started with the pilots and the cabin crew and blessed the airport staff. Even Lennox got mentioned for driving us to Long Bay safely. I was hungrier than I first realised having only eaten plane food at lunchtime. Mother Morgan has put on an amazing spread of food that could feed an army. My plate is full of curry goat, fried dumplings, ackee and saltfish, fried plantain, steamed callaloo and rice and peas. My eyes are clearly bigger than my stomach because I cannot finish it and jet lag is winning, reminding me of the time difference. I leave Esther with her grandmother, intending to lie down and rest my eyes for a few minutes. I do not wake up until the following morning. It does not matter what time you go to sleep in the Caribbean or how tired you are, when you hear the Morgan's cockerel crowing, you automatically wake up.

10 ~ PATTI

I am bawling down the phone crying my eyes out and I know I am scaring the hell out of Ann, but I cannot help it. I have been crying since Marcus left my home about half an hour ago.

"For goodness sake Patti, what on earth is wrong?" begs Ann, but I cannot speak to answer her back. "Is something wrong with Yolanda?"

I manage a weak answer, "No."

"Ok is everything ok with Auntie Veronica?"

"As far as I know she's fine," I answer.

"Then for the love of God Patti, speak to me or we're getting in the car and coming over right now!" Ann threatens.

I sigh deeply and say, "Its Marcus, his dad passed away last night in Jamaica."

I can hear Ann exhaling over the phone, and I am sure I hear her kiss her teeth.

"Really Patti? Really? Whilst I am sorry to hear about

the passing of Marcus' dad, are you really over there crying your heart out over a man you just met whose father died. A father whom you did not meet? You need to get a grip, Patti!"

"It's the way he found out" I interrupt "We had such a lovely night out and he stayed over at my house..." shoot, why did I tell her that?

"Damn Patti, Marcus stayed at your house? That's a bit soon isn't it? How long have you been dating him now? A couple of weeks?" Ann quizzes.

"Three months as a matter of fact" I respond. "And while we were getting it on his father was taking his final breath!"

"Ok, Patti I did not mean to upset you more than you already are! Where is Marcus now?" Ann begins to sound as though she sympathises, so I calm down too.

"Oh, he's gone to see his older brother, and then he's grabbing some clothes and coming back here. I did not want him to be on his own tonight".

I can tell Ann is probably biting through her tongue so as not to say anything disapproving.

She simply says, "Ok den, we'll catch up properly at 'Westfield Wednesday' this week. Bye Patti, take care and send my condolences to Marcus."

I put my phone to charge and I try to keep myself busy until Marcus returns. I have another shower and change into a pair of tracksuit bottoms and an Island Girls Rock T-shirt. I then change the bed linen and put the sheets and duvet cover into the washing machine in the laundry room downstairs. I load the dishwasher and wipe down the kitchen units. I sit at the dining room table going through my diary to check what I have coming up at work next week and I can see at a glance a very busy week is unfolding in front of me.

After years of speculation, the probation service has just divided into two separate organisations, one to remain in the public sector and the other going to the private sector. I have been sifted to remain in the public sector, however, as I have already worked as a civil servant, I put in for a transfer to London Probation Service (LPS) in the private sector. Throughout that period of transition, I have supported colleagues in my team to manage the changes and in February 2015, the London Probation Service was sold to a private company, that none of us had heard of before.

It soon became apparent that the company was well established in the states delivering services in prisons in the US. Everybody has their personal reservations about the private criminal justice sector, but I am looking forward to working in new ways and moving away from bureaucracy and endless paperwork. I am particularly looking forward to using new IT systems and working in partnership with agencies specialising in housing, substance misuses and mental health services. Monday morning is going to be the launch of the new 'cohort model' and I have expressed an interest in managing a team of women probation officers in the Women's cohort. For the first time in the history of the probation service, we are able exclusively to develop services for women run by women and I am excited about my role again.

For my sins, I have also kept my hand in running groups and worked as a sessional programme tutor running the Integrated Domestic Abuse Programme (IDAP) for the last six years. I enjoyed delivering the programme alongside members of the IDAP team, the fact they were willing to pay me too was a bonus, but I would have run it for free. I was privileged to hear the stories the men told me about the first time they witnessed domestic violence when they were children and equally privileged to witness the men change their longstanding entrenched views on women. 'Lightbulb' moments I call them; when the world they lived in finally began to make sense.

I was so good at creating the environment for the men to talk freely and safely challenge their behaviour that a segment of one of my sessions that I was co-facilitating, was used to train up new magistrates. I could not have been more delighted with the recognition. I can see I am down to run a group on Thursday evening at the Ilford office and for the first time in six years, I want to cancel, as I am already exhausted from the weekend. But I know that I won't cancel and let my colleagues down and I know I will enjoy the group once I get there. If I am right, we are due to cover sexual abuse at the next session, not my favourite session but an integral part of the programme that needs to be tackled with sensitivity.

It is shaping up to be an incredibly long day, but I thought maybe Marcus could meet me after work and we could go for a meal at Ginger Sky again. I update my diary to include meeting up with Ann on Wednesday evening and the fact that Marcus will probably be leaving for Jamaica on Friday. I plan on taking him to the airport and countdown the days until he returns in three weeks' time.

It is well after midnight when Marcus returns with a travelling bag of clothes. I am ironing a shirt to wear to work when I hear his knock at the door. He looks absolutely shattered with the sparkle clearly gone from his eyes and he doesn't look in the mood for small talk. I hold him by the hand and take him upstairs to unpack his case. I clear a side on the vanity unit, and I place his toiletry bag on the right-hand side. His 'Man Bag' looks out of place in my all white bathroom as no man has ever stayed in my home before. When I close the en-suite door, I see that Marcus is fast asleep on my bed and I spend the next hour organising my clothes for the following week.

In the morning, Marcus drops me off at my office on St Johns Street and I know Beverley the receptionist sees Marcus kissing me as he leaves. By the time I get into the office and sign in, I am confident that everybody on the ground floor knows about it too. I would not be surprised if I found that Beverley told everyone in the whole building by tannoy that I had a drop dead gorgeous man drop me off at work. The staff on the ground floor would not dare ask me my personal business. Hardly any of them acknowledge me as I walk through the office anyway, as they are now in the National Probation Service and would not talk to their colleagues in the LPS. They think that they are a cut above us. The LPS staff are situated in an open plan office on the first floor of the building. I make my way upstairs and I hastily walk across the floor saying good morning to my team before going into my office. I soon re-emerge with my mug to make my second cup of ginger tea of the day. My team knows better than to approach me before I've had my morning cuppa and a chance to check my mail. I open a letter from HR recruitment confirming that I have not been successful at interview for promotion. I huff, shake my head then switch into autopilot and get on with my day. At lunchtime, I pop into the supermarket and pick up some toiletries for Marcus and I eat the salad that he prepared for me that morning.

I speak to Yolanda on the phone before going into a one to one supervision with a member of my team. Of all the tasks I have as a middle manager, supervision is my favourite task. I enjoy listening to my team members talk about their cases and discussing the approaches they are planning to take to manage risk and rehabilitate their service users. I still believe that my job is to assist and support my team to make defensible decisions and protect the public from harm.

It is way after 4 pm by the time we wrap up the

supervision session and I am ready to go home. I call Marcus to check he is on his way. However, when he arrives the whole office knows about it. He is escorted upstairs by Beverley who leads the way like she is a plus size supermodel, and she keeps winking at me! Marcus is wearing a grey suit and holding a bouquet of at least two dozen yellow roses, my favourite.

"Good Afternoon Empress, these are for you and thank you for everything you did for me last night!" I know he is talking about his dad passing, but Beverley and the rest of my team are clearly thinking of something else. As I take my coat from the stand, I blush and attempt to leave the office. I can hear the whispers behind my back as I walk across the room. Although I'm embarrassed on the outside, deep down I feel chuffed with all the attention. "Wait until I tell Ann all about this!" I thought.

11~ CHARMAINE

I really have the best mum in the world, not only has she agreed to look after my babies for four weeks so I can accompany Junior to Jamaica, she has also given me her pardoner hand so I will have spending money whilst I am there.

A pardoner club is a Caribbean informal savings club, a bit like one of those Christmas saving clubs, but with no hampers at Christmastime. They were very popular back when banks would not give loans to Caribbean people when they first arrived in the UK. A lot of people were able to buy their homes and furniture with their pardoner money, so my Mum tells me. I promptly go up the Westfield to look for my friend who works at Primark to help me to choose a few clothes for my holiday, I mean for the funeral. Thankfully, the summer season is coming to an end and most of the clothes are reduced in the sales. I stop at the market stall to buy two pairs of wedge-heeled sandals, and I stop again at

Superdrug and buy a bottle of sunscreen lotion and insect repellent. I am already dreading the prospect of being eaten alive by the mosquitoes and sand flies. But I can't lie I am looking forward to going away for my own selfish reasons. You see when we got married; Junior told our guests that we were going on honeymoon to Jamaica to meet his parents. We got as far as the airport where Junior let me know he was an over-stayer and could not leave the country until he sorted out his paperwork. I was blue vex. We spent our first night as man and wife at a hotel near the airport, with the promise that when his paperwork was sorted out, we would travel to see them. That was nearly five years ago and now we are finally going for his dad's funeral. We have spoken to his folks on the phone and we sent photos of the twins, but they have not seen the twins in the flesh yet and his dad never will.

I am not looking forward to seeing Rose as she looks down on me and Junior. She does not approve of Junior's lifestyle. Junior was a weed smoker when I met him, and he's been smoking weed throughout our marriage. I doubt he's going to stop smoking weed now. It's part of him and the people he hangs with. I ain't going to lie, I enjoyed a puff or two when we first started hanging out, but I stopped all of that when I was preggers with the twins. It is the first thing Junior thinks about when he wakes up in the morning and the last thing he does before he goes to sleep. Most of the money from his record sales went on weed for him and his so-called friends but I stopped them from smoking it here in my home. To be honest Junior has cut down dramatically on the weed smoking, as he does not want to get stopped at the airport when he's travelling; I hope he's able to stop smoking altogether after staying in his parents' home.

When I get back to Mum's her order from the JD Williams catalogue has just arrived and to my delight, my Mum has ordered me new underwear, PJs and a swimsuit and she loans me a suitcase. I can't thank my Mum enough and I say a tearful goodbye to her and the twins, who have no idea that this is the last time they'll see me for a while. I am so sorry that I cannot afford to take them with me. They have never had a holiday; not even to Spain. However, I am glad for the time away with Junior to decide what we want from this marriage. In my opinion, the ball is in Junior's court. I pull the suitcase on its wheels around the corner and Marcia ushers me into her flat. She has a pile of clothes for me and stacks of miniature toiletries consisting of deodorant, baby oil, shower gels and shampoo, I have no idea where they came from, but I am grateful, and I take them all the same.

I plan to wear the same black suit that I wore to court to the funeral with the black wedge heel sandals I got in the market. Once indoors I pack my suitcase leaving out a denim, blue jumpsuit and jacket to wear to the airport. I pack my new handbag with my sunglasses, travel money, our passports and tickets. I remember my Mum saying to pack some underwear and a change of clothes in my bag just in case my luggage goes missing, which I dutifully do. Behind me, I hear Junior booking a cab to take us to the airport the following day.

Apparently, we're meeting Marcus at the airport in the departure lounge. To be honest, I welcome the opportunity to catch up with Marcus, as we did not get the chance to really speak at the court. Marcus helped me to buy the house in Plaistow, but it caused a big bust-up between Junior and Marcus because Marcus insisted the property was put in my name. I recall Marcus seeing the twins once at the hospital when they were born and Junior was really rude to him, accusing Marcus of stealing his money. However, nuff time has passed and

Marcus held out the olive branch by coming to court to support Junior, so it was water under the bridge. I hope Junior can be civil on the 10-hour flight to Jamaica and not fall out with Marcus mid-air.

On arrival at the airport, Junior goes into big shot mode; like he is some big-time reggae artist accustomed to international first class travel all the time. The check-in clerk insists she can upgrade us to Premium Economy but not First Class and Junior is about to let his feelings be known until I remind him I don't care where we sit, I just feel blessed to be getting on a plane for the first time! He prances through the duty-free area smiling at people who have no clue who he is, and he soon notices. I have money to buy a bottle of perfume for my Mum and two bottles of Baileys. I love my drink, and something tells me I am going to need something to take the edge off things whilst we're staying at Junior's parents' home.

Junior and I end up at one of the restaurants that serve an all-day breakfast. I know he is not keen to eat there given the number of pork items on the menu. I order eggs benedict with fresh orange juice. I figure I want to try something new. Junior looks at me like I am trying to play posh, but I ignore him. In fact, I am getting very good at ignoring his snide comments and put-downs. Junior orders toast and a hot chocolate, which is probably the best thing he can do. When breakfast arrives, he tries to rush me stating he has a plane to catch, to which I ask him if he's flying the plane. I know he does not like me back chatting him, so we continue to eat our breakfast in silence.

Eventually, we plod through to the departure lounge, which is already full of people excited about travelling to Jamaica. I wave over at Marcus and he ushers us over to the two seats he has been saving. His dreadlocks are now down on his back and he is sporting a new goatee, which I don't recall seeing at the court a week ago. He gives me a huge cuddle and compliments me on my weight loss. I am delighted, it is so noticeable. The brothers greet each other warmly again and I am relieved there's no tension there. They sit and talk about their father and I can see tears in both of their eyes. I am truly touched by the warmth between them. In my opinion, this is precisely how the brothers should be; close, especially at a time like this. I hope that this closeness will continue long after the trip has ended, Marcus and Junior have been estranged for way too long. From what I can overhear a date for the funeral has already been set as well as a Homegoing celebration at the house and Junior has been requested to sing his father's favourite hymn; Blessed Assurance. With all of Junior's dancehall and reggae ways, even I know he will do the song justice and give his dad the send-off he deserves. Manley will read the Eulogy as he is the older brother and Marcus will be the Master of Ceremony at the Homegoing Celebration. Junior is clearly impressed with what he's heard so far and he nods in agreement. There's a nice reflective pause between them, both men comfortable in each other's company. Junior asks about the will and Marcus says he heard there'll be a reading of the will at some point during our stay. Again, Junior nods indicating that he is safe with what's been said.

"I missed you bruv!" Junior said,

"I missed you too man" Marcus replied.

Over the tannoy, the check-in staff request that the following passengers come to the front desk and I am surprised to hear Marcus' name. When he comes back, he tells us he's been upgraded to First Class. He grabs his bags and says he'll see us on the other side. I can tell Junior is proper vex, but he keeps it down as he does not want Marcus to see how vex he is right now. Deep down I am chuckling with laughter. Here we go back to fucking square one.

12 ~ ROSE

Marcus enters the room swoops up Esther like he won the lottery and thanks us for having his child for him. Everybody laughs. He kisses Esther on the cheek and congratulates me and Manley on our bundle of joy. Junior and Charmaine come inside next and I stand up to greet them. Junior looks exactly the same, but Charmaine, she looks wonderful, she's clearly half the size that she was when I saw her last. As I give her a hug, I whisper in her ear telling her how good she looks, and she returns the compliment stating that I don't look like I have just had a baby. There's a lot of love in the room as Junior, Charmaine and Marcus greet everybody and the sombre mood in the room lifts momentarily.

The suitcases are retrieved by the menfolk of the house and Junior and Marcus bring out all the items from the suitcases that their mum had requested. Marcus has put together a video celebration of their father's life, which he would like the family to vet before the Homegoing Celebration. Mother Morgan sits everybody down and Medina, the help, fetches cold drinks for everyone. We all then listen to Mother Morgan talk about her husband's final moments and there isn't a dry eye in the house. Lennox and Medina are standing nearby and are sobbing hard too. Pops Morgan simply died in his sleep. He had influenza but he was making a recovery. Manley takes the lead and instructs the family to hold hands as he starts to pray for strength during the days and weeks ahead. We all then get ready to make the journey to the funeral home in Negril.

I am not certain where the big yellow school bus has come from but when I go outside with Esther, I am glad to see it as it means we can all travel to Negril together. Charmaine sits next to me and we have a wonderful chat as we drive at speed up and down some dirt roads until we get to the main road. I point out places of interest until it's obvious I am boring her, so I switch up the conversation and I ask her about Gary and Gaby. She lightens up and gives me a marathon update on their progress and I am so pleased to hear they are doing so well. When she shows me photos of the twins on her mobile phone, I tear up, Gary is the spitting image of his dad and Gaby looks so beautiful just like her mum. I cannot help feeling so ashamed that I have not kept in touch, which has resulted in the twins not knowing me, Manley or our girls. I am not a fan of Junior's but that should not stop me from getting closer to Charmaine. Since Pops passed, I am acutely aware that family is more important than anything else, so I promise myself that I will do better when we return to the UK, regardless of the beef between Manley and Junior. I invite Charmaine, her mother and the family over to our home next month and I plan to pull out all the stops to welcome them back into the family fold.

It is almost dusk when we reach the chapel of rest, we all pile out of the bus to stretch our legs, and thankfully, we arrive just in time to see the sunset behind the beautiful waves. I will try to put into words what happens when we all enter the tiny chapel of rest. There is no waiting area like I was hoping for, there are a few rows of chairs on either side of the room and at the end of the room is Pops Morgan laid out in a chocolate brown casket. There is no way for me to avoid seeing him as everyone goes straight toward the coffin, everybody begins to cry and wail. Charmaine just about gets to

Junior before he falls, and Manley and Marcus hold on to each other and sob their hearts out. By the time I get to the front I take over from Marcus and I hold onto Manley. Marcus goes to cuddle his mum, and I can't help but wish he had a significant other in his life.

Once we have all cried until we can cry no more, Mother Morgan asks Manley to pray and we file silently back to the school bus. As if on autopilot, the bus is driven to a local Jerk Hut set up on the roadside. As we leave the bus the smoke from the Jerk Pan stings my eyes, so I shield Esther's face and we quickly find free seats furthest away from the smoke. We are almost on the beach and the cool Caribbean breeze is blowing in the opposite direction. This is a lovely spot and it looks quite popular with the locals and tourists alike. I feed Esther and give her a nappy change, whilst the menfolk go to order some food to take back to the house.

I sit on a bench looking out to the horizon of the Caribbean Sea, the sun is rapidly changing the skyline from yellow to orange then from orange to indigo followed closely by purple. The last remaining swimmers make their way to shore. I can see a group of boys hurrying to finish off the last overs of their cricket match with flair as they hit sixes into the sea. I can now see that the bathers are three girls about 9 to 10 years old, not much older than my eldest daughter Mary but they look older. They cover themselves with their towels but the one in front, the leader drops her towel in front of the boys to reveal her bikini showing off her tiny breasts.

She's got that 'forced ripe' air about her, sticking out her prepubescent breasts and her backside as she walks by. Fortunately, the older boys pay her no mind as they pack away their makeshift cricket stumps, grab their belongings and make their way up the beach towards the Jerk Hut. Not getting the attention she desires she leads her crew in the direction of the adult men who are waiting to be served, thankfully, they pay her no mind either. She clearly thinks she's grown; lord help us when she's a bit older. I wouldn't buy a bikini for my children to wear, I say to myself judgementally, let children be children for as long as possible, they have their whole lives to be adults. But the scene does remind me of growing up in Jamaica and the long summers I spent with Uncle Samuel, his wife beautiful Auntie Myrtle and their two daughters Jestina and Paulina.

As soon as school was out for eight weeks, I had my bags packed ready to visit my cousins. Jestina was my age and her sister was two years younger than us. Uncle

Samuel was my Dad's only brother 11 months his senior, he was a retired businessman having made his fortune during the late 40s and early 50s. After the second world war, a lot of Jamaicans who stayed on in America and the United Kingdom arranged to sell their family land in Jamaica. They had no intention of coming back to Jamaica, so Uncle Samuel became rich very quickly especially when developers wanted the land to build hotels and beachfront properties. He bought a former plantation house in May Pen in the parish of Clarendon, a beautiful five bedroom property set in five acres of lush green landscape and I'm positive every fruit imaginable was there. My cousins even had an outhouse that was renovated into a castle with a shallow moat around it. My cousins and I could easily jump over into the shade of the castle where we would play with our dolls or play games. The castle was really special.

Uncle Samuel caught his own fish, as my Mum would say, which meant he married his secretary and they worked together until they retired. Auntie Myrtle was a stunningly beautiful woman admired throughout the district and she'd had several suitors and marriage proposals. This was not surprising because she was beautiful with flawless brown skin and long jet-black 'coolie' hair. The perfect mix of African and Indian heritage. After working late one evening at the office, Uncle Samuel gave her a lift to Bible study, and he proposed in the car. Auntie Myrtle always said she had to wait a whole two years for him to propose, but she would have waited for him forever. She said yes but she stipulated when they got married, Uncle Samuel would join her at the Baptist church in May Pen and he duly complied.

Sunday mornings in their household comprised of us rising early eating a hearty breakfast prepared by the kitchen maids and getting ready for church. In the background, I recalled a Jim Reeves album being played from the stereogram. That would be the only music that was allowed to be played on a Sunday. I would sit at the back of the car with my cousins in our Sunday school clothes and best Sunday school shoes, trying not to mess up my hairdo. Auntie Myrtle had just combed through our hair, applied hair grease then parted it down the centre into two ponytails with multiple white ribbons. All we had to do was stay pristine until we got to church. She would turn to us sternly in the car as we approached the church car park and warn us saying "The church is watching us. You are a reflection of us, and we are a reflection of you."

People who were visitors to the church often mistook us for triplets such was the resemblance. We did not correct them either, we simply smiled. Uncle Samuel was the church usher, therefore it was important for us to be at church in good time for him to open the building before everybody else arrived. Auntie Myrtle would retrieve the freshly picked flowers she had picked from her garden, hibiscus I recall, to arrange a floral display at the altar. Our job was to put a copy of the hymnal on every seat including those upstairs in the mezzanine. After which Uncle Samuel showed us to our seats. Then, he would put on his white gloves and position himself at the entrance of the church.

I smile to myself at the memory of Uncle Samuel smiling warmly as he welcomed visitors to the house of the Lord. He still holds this position in the church today, although at 90 and with a cane, he may walk a little slower. He still has all of his pearly white teeth and a full head of black hair, but I have long suspected that Uncle Samuel dyes his hair jet black to match his ageless wife's hair, but that is the only thing vain about him. Despite his wealth, he is warm, generous, humble and down to earth. He sponsored my Dad when he wanted to come up to the mother country to seek work, and he paid for my Mum and I to travel by air to England to join my Dad that September.

I loved everything about being at this church. The building was modern and welcoming with a hall at the back for functions and rooms upstairs for prayer meetings and other church meetings. The rostrum housed an organ and a standalone drum kit that was longing for someone to jump into the seat and play it. I was satisfied playing the tambourine my cousins taught me to play. I loved the praise and worship session, the Sunday school teachings, the sermons and the choir singing, it was a world away from the Catholic Church I attended occasionally with my parents.

Despite the church being in the Caribbean, I often felt the old Catholic church was drafty and cold. I went to confession, but as a child, I felt I had nothing to confess, so I would make stories up instead like, I took sugar from the larder cupboard or I wasted the butter on my hard dough bread. The priest would give me a couple of Hail Marys to recite and then I was out of there absolved of my sins. At 10 years old, it all felt like I was going through the motions with no real conviction as everything went through the priest. I had never even seen a Bible! Auntie

Myrtle was the Sunday school teacher for our age group and her drills for remembering our memory verses were interactive and competitive. It was normally girls vs. boys and on average, the girls brought home the Golden Cup most weeks. I think having Jestina and Paulina on your team meant we had an advantage over the boys.

After hearing me sing one evening Auntie Myrtle put me forward to audition for the solo in the choir and I was selected. Church gossip at the time was that I only got the solo because I was the choir mistress's niece and she was criticised quite a bit because I was Catholic and not a born-again Christian but Auntie Myrtle advocated that I had auditioned fairly and squarely like everybody else and my voice suited the particular rendition of the song. In the coming weeks, I was to practice with her every evening when she came in from work and Jestina and Paulina were my backing singers. We loved practising in front of the mirror in the living room pretending we were the Grace Thrillers until we almost lost our voices.

One of the highlights of the church calendar during the summer was our annual coach trip to Hellshire beach in the south of the island. Preparations for the excursion would start the night before with Auntie Myrtle instructing her staff to prepare the church picnic. There was always mountains of food, more than enough to feed the whole congregation. My cousins and I had our jobs too, we stole the desserts escaped to the doll's house and shared the spoils with each other.

The following day we rose early to meet at the church, the atmosphere was electrifying with the excitement of 40 children and their parents, grandparents and extended families, even my parents showed up. When the coaches set off the choruses began led by Auntie Myrtle who had replaced her elaborate wide-brimmed church hat with a bright multi-coloured headscarf.

She marched up and down the coach singing, "What do you think about Jesus?"

We would respond, "He's alright." clapping back gleefully. The tambourines and African drumbeat kept everyone in time, with a background of chorus after joyful chorus it took under an hour to get there but when you're a child, it seemed to take forever.

Hellshire beach has to be my favourite beach in all of Jamaica. The sea is crystal clear, and the sand is almost white. Everybody helped set up the picnic in the spot they thought would offer the most shade from the relentless sun. Pastor Maurice prayed then we ate. We, the children, ate as quickly as we could as we were longing to dive into the warm Caribbean water. Only to be told to wait and let the food digest or run the risk of getting a bellyache. We all had our costumes on underneath our clothes so as soon as the all-clear was given I raced my cousins and the other children taking off my clothes and running into the sea. Auntie Myrtle shouting after us, not to get our hair wet, but it was already too late, as we misjudged the depth of the water and plunged under the water. I can still remember the shock and defeated look on her face. I chuckle out loud at the good memories. We spent the whole all day on the beach playing cricket, tag and cooling off in the sea until it was time to go home, all the way back home sitting on our towels, with sand plastered on our dry skin and entangled in our hair, we sang rousing choruses.

Once we got back home, Auntie Myrtle escorted us around the back of the property, and we entered the house through the service entrance. We slipped off our sandals and beachwear on the bathroom door whilst Auntie ran us a hot bath. I'm surprised there was any sand left at Hellshire beach because the majority of it was scattered around the floor. Someone was going to have to scrape it up and send it back. Jestina bathed first concentrating on washing her blossoming body whilst Auntie focused on washing her long jet-black hair. After two washes with shampoo, Auntie signalled to Jestina that her time was up as she emptied and cleaned the bathtub. Auntie repeated this three times singing the same song until we were all clean.

After drying off and creaming our skin with cocoa butter, we emerged like angels from our bedroom dressed in our long cotton nightdresses with the hems almost touching the ground. The chest area was padded and had long sleeves. They were very fashionable at the time, Jestina's was blue, Paulina's pink and mine was yellow. One by one sitting on a dining room chair in the TV room, Auntie combed through our thick hair and dried it using the hairdryer. It was new but not as technical as nowadays. This hairdryer only had one setting, which was extremely hot. So hot, we had to hold down the tops of our ears to prevent them from getting burnt. Normally we never ceased from chatting but having spent the whole day at the beach playing and laughing we just wanted to get this whole hair process to be over with and go to bed. After our hair was bone dry and manageable Auntie parted and greased Jestina's hair. Auntie was tired standing, so she commanded Jestina to grab a cushion and sit crossed legged on the floor between her legs whilst she made herself comfortable on the sofa.

Paulina and I sat in one of the old cane rockers trying not to fall asleep. Uncle Samuel came in after packing away all of the picnic stuff, and asked if we wanted hot chocolate which was a silly question because we always said yes! Then he affectionately asked Auntie if she wanted tea-tea, coffee-tea, ginger tea or coco-tea. She laughed wearily and asked him for a cup of cocoa-tea too. Paulina and I followed him to the kitchen and sat at the table to watch him make our drinks at the stove.

He looked worn out by the day's excursion to the beach too, but his trademark smile and winks were still there. He warmed condensed milk into a large saucepan with water then he added sugar, nutmeg, cinnamon leaves and several coco balls. Whilst the mixture was bubbling away, Uncle removed two old milo tins from the cupboard that had long since been converted into jugs with handles and he placed them on the kitchen table. He then went into the pantry and he came back with the largest loaf of bun I have ever seen. Using the bread knife, he expertly cut five extra thick slices. Paulina and I ate the crumbs quickly trying not to get cut. I fetched butter and sliced cheese from the fridge as instructed and Paulina and I assembled the bun and cheese sandwiches. Uncle returned to the stove removed the cinnamon sticks and poured the tea into one of the milo tins. He turned to us smiling with the hot tea in one tin and the empty tin in the other. Now, this was the bit we wanted to watch. Uncle poured tea from a height from one tin to the other repeatedly, an old-fashioned way of cooling the tea down catching the breeze from the slightly opened kitchen window. A skill he had observed his maternal grandmother and his mother do and I would do for my girls. Paulina and I were mesmerized. When he was satisfied the tea was ready and would not burn our delicate lips and tongue using a sieve he poured the tea into five assorted mugs on a tray and we carried the sandwiches into the other room.

By the time we got back to the TV room Auntie had just finished plaiting Jestina's hair and was placing an old nylon stocking over her head to keep the style in place during the night. Uncle switched on the new television to watch the Evangelist, Jimmy Swaggart's latest sermon from America. Auntie had a few sips from her tea nodding her head in agreement with whatever the Evangelist was hollering about before calling me to take up Jestina's position on the floor for the final process. I still had my tea and bun and cheese in my hand carefully taking sips of my tea and biting into my sandwich, whilst she was trying to tame my mane. I was fearful that if I put my sandwich down one of my cousins would gobble it up before I had a chance to protest. That was my last summer in Jamaica before leaving to join my father in London. It was bittersweet because I missed my father, but I was going to miss my Uncle and my cousins even more. There were promises made that I could come back for the holidays, but I knew deep down that wasn't going to happen.

The next time I saw them was when they came to our wedding, Jestina and Paulina were my bridesmaids. Uncle Samuel was proud as punch and he gave such an emotional speech. Before we slipped away to go on our honeymoon, he gave me a cheque for the deposit on our new home. I sobbed silent tears when I thought about it. Uncle Samuel loved me like he loved his own daughters and he still does.

Mother Morgan isn't crying anymore she is speaking with Charmaine and she sounds quite light-hearted. I tune out of their conversation and tune into the sweet reggae music from the nearby sound system. Thankfully, it's not that awful dancehall rubbish, but proper reggae music that I remember growing up with, artists like Ken Boothe and John Holt. My Dad had a wide collection of vinyl 45 records that he started when he first came to London from Jamaica. It was the only treat to himself after working 12-hour shifts starting work at six in the morning. He should have finished at 2 pm, but he never turned down the opportunity to work overtime when it was on offer. When he got paid he would travel down to Brixton and come home with the latest reggae single from Jamaica and a bar of chocolate for me and we would dance away whilst Mum made Saturday soup and cussed everybody for not helping her out. Dad gave his collection away when he became a born-again Christian, but reggae music still reminds me of my upbringing and good family times.

Manley comes over calling my name, interrupting my thoughts,

"Rosie? You have any money?"

"Yeah sure, go in my purse; I think I have some US dollars," I reply.

Then I remember that I left my contraceptive pills in my purse and I think I am going to throw up thinking about what could happen once Manley discovers my secret. Although it's dark, the light from the fire in the

Jerk Pan lights up his face as he looks up at me holding the sachet containing my pill.

"What in God's name is this Rose?"

13 ~ PATTI

When we get indoors I am surprised to find the dining room table is set for two, and whatever Marcus has cooked in my absence smells delicious. He takes my coat and he tells me to sit at the table. Marcus has made curried lamb with Jamaican rice and peas and a fresh green salad and it all tastes delicious. Yolanda comes in unexpectedly and while she greets me with a kiss, Marcus fetches her a plate and serves her some food. My daughter eats the food like she's never eaten before, she even picks up the bone and starts sucking the marrow out of it.

Marcus and I both stare at her and when she notices, she simply says, "What? The food tastes good Man; Marcus cooks better than you Mum!"

The pattern continues on Tuesday with Marcus making my lunch and dropping it off at work and then him coming up to my office escorted by Beverley. Today's bouquet is a dozen yellow roses and a cheeky smile. Once again, when I get indoors Marcus has cooked jerk chicken, macaroni cheese and corn on the cob. He has set the table for three just in case Yolanda comes home. On 'Westfield Wednesday' he even drops me off to meet up with Ann and he makes me promise to call him when I am ready to leave because he will be in the area picking up his suit for his dad's funeral. It looks like today is the day that Marcus and Ann will finally meet, and I am very nervous about how Ann will behave.

I arrive early at our usual meeting point and after a few minutes, Ann arrives looking lovely, as ever. We greet each other as usual, although it does feel a bit awkward, as we have not spoken since my meltdown on the telephone when we found out about Marcus' dad passing. We head for the Mac store on the lower floor as I am looking to replenish and refresh my makeup. I never want to be in a position where I have run out. After I make my purchase, we head to Forever 21 as Ann wants to find a cardigan or jacket to wear under her gown at court. She's been working at the crown court and finds the building quite cold. Unfortunately, she does not see anything she likes so we decide to get something to eat.

Well after her behaviour a couple of months ago we are banned from the Italian restaurant, so we head towards Levi Root's new 'Rastaraunt' and fortunately we walk straight in and are seated in a booth. I must say the décor looks really authentic and the music is set at just the right volume for you to appreciate it and still have a decent catch up without having to compete with the rhythmic sounds. The menu looks good too, something from every island in the Caribbean so I order the Bajan style fishcakes, the curry goat and rice. Ann orders the chicken soup, sea bass with festivals and plantain.

Levi spots Ann, he comes over and they greet each other warmly. I recall Ann telling me that his company will be catering for Eli's blessing next month. Levi warmly greets me too and I congratulate him on his latest business venture. I am grinning like a Cheshire cat because Ann knows that I have been a fan of Levi Roots from the first time I saw him slay the Dragon's on Dragon's Den. I have all of his recipe books at home. I pretended they were for Yolanda but she's more interested in eating food not cooking it! I even queued up outside a bookshop in Croydon for him to sign two of them, so meeting him in person again and getting my photo taken with him is a real treat. Ann rolls her eyes at me when she sees me updating my social networking sites before we even finish our meals.

"So, tell me girlfriend, how is Marcus bearing up?" Ann asks.

I sense she sincerely wants to know, and she made the effort to ask so I update her about Marcus staying with me until he leaves for Jamaica on Saturday. Ann's body language is on point, she nods and sighs in the right places and appears delighted to hear about Marcus dropping me to work, bringing me flowers and cooking for me at home.

"Well I am really happy for you Patti; the flowers stuff is a bit naff, but he sounds like a nice man; I can't wait to meet him."

"Well you won't have long to wait," I reply, "he's picking me up when we're done."

"Oh!" She exclaims, then asks our attentive waiter for the drink's menu and orders herself a strong drink.

I am surprised, Ann does not usually drink alcohol when she has an important day at court and when she does drink, it's a glass of Rosé, not rum. My anxiety levels go through the roof, so I text Marcus to join us before the alcohol has a chance to hit her system. When 'Mister Man' arrives, he is carrying a lovely bouquet of flowers and after giving me a kiss on the lips he turns to Ann, as she looks up she drops her glass spilling her drink across the table.

"Oh shite!" She mutters.

I'm not sure if she's swearing over spilling her drink or swearing at Marcus.

On the other hand, Marcus is as cool as a cucumber, he steps back to avoid getting alcohol on his suit then motions a waitress to clean our table. Without missing a step, he says, "Hi," and hands the flowers to Ann, "These flowers are for you Queen Antoinette; I have been really looking forward to meeting you. Patti has told me so much about you!"

Antoinette then blushes and says, "Young man come and sit right beside me and tell me if you have any older brothers who are FINE just like you?!" They both laugh out loud and I am relieved that they like each other. Marcus orders another round of drinks including a soft drink for himself. We make small talk and every now and then Marcus looks at me across the table and winks. Marcus really holds his own as Ann grills him and asks him about a million questions like he's giving evidence in the witness box. When she asks if the sex is good, I try to interrupt but Marcus laughs and says that I'm a good teacher! On that note, I hit Ann on her hand for asking rude questions and I request the bill. Whilst we're waiting for our bill, Marcus says he has a surprise for me, which gets our full attention.

"Patti, I wanted to thank you for everything you've done for me over the last week. Your thoughtful kindness is something I'll never forget. To show you my appreciation, this is for you," he hands me a white envelope. I don't really like surprises, but I am curious and puzzled about what's inside.

"Shall I open it now?" I ask Marcus.

"Of course, you can and hurry up about it too," Ann answers for him and he nods.

When I open the envelope, I see the Virgin Atlantic Logo in the top left-hand corner, and I gasp. Marcus has bought me a plane ticket to Jamaica. Ann gasps too and I can tell she's impressed. I am silent and a bit taken aback. I can sense Marcus is disappointed by my reaction and I start to explain. "Marcus, darling this is a wonderful gift, but I cannot accept it, I have not booked any leave next week and I have Yolanda, I would not want to be away from her for two whole weeks."

"Patti," he replies, "everything's been taken care of."

"Hun, I'm really confused, what do you mean?" I ask.

"Your colleague Beverley has been in on this surprise all along, she contacted your manager and she has given you the time off!"

"Really?" I say. I can feel myself getting emotional. "But what about Yolanda? I know she's hardly at home, but she is my responsibility!"

Marcus gives me another envelope and when I see another plane ticket in Yolanda's name, I burst into tears at the table. Ann orders another round of drinks and tells me to fix up!

We get up early Friday morning to take Marcus to the airport. Not that we slept much. Marcus was fretting about travelling to Jamaica with his brother Junior. He said Junior was a live wire and although they had seen each other recently you never knew which Junior was going to show up. He was like Jekyll and Hyde. His wife, Charmaine, on the other hand, was very nice and he was looking forward to introducing her and the rest of the family to Yolanda and I once the funeral was over. His mother was already aware I was coming, and she was looking forward to meeting us. On my way back from the Gatwick airport, I called Yolanda to say we needed to visit her grandmother to break the news that we were going to Jamaica on Monday. Yolanda was groaning down the phone but said she would be up by the time I got back, so we could go and shop for our holiday. I did a quick food shop locally and Yolanda and I drove to Lakeside to grab a few end of season bargains.

By the time I got to Veronica's it was already after one in the afternoon. Veronica had her head tied with a bit of material with the familiar smell of Bay Rum which I inhaled as I greeted her with a kiss and a hug.

"Hi, Nan!" Yolanda said giving her grandmother a kiss, "what's happening aren't you well?" She inquires.

"Yeah, Mum are you alright?"

We followed her down the hall to the kitchen pausing to take off our outdoor shoes and coats.

"I don't feel myself today, I've had this headache since this morning," she said sadly.

"I'm sorry to hear that Mum. Have you taken anything for it?" I ask.

"Well you know me, Patti, I'll try and work on it myself before I take painkillers," she mumbled, "wanna cup of tea you two?"

Yolanda had already left the kitchen and switched on the TV.

"Yes please, Mum I'm parched, but I'll make it, you go and sit down,"

Mum obediently pulls out a dining chair and sits down. I walk around the kitchen on autopilot. I know this kitchen really well because I grew up here. I discard the water in the kettle and refill it with fresh water. I notice Veronica has lamb defrosting in a bowl in the sink alongside a juicy piece of pigtail.

"Mum! Are you making soup today or tomorrow?" I say praying it's for this evening's dinner. Saturday soup is my favourite Barbadian meal and Veronica makes the best soup in the world. I start salivating at the thought of it.

"Well, I was going to make it tomorrow, but I can make it for you this afternoon?" Mum perked up. "If any leave back, you could get some tomorrow as well,"

"Good idea Mum I'll help you," I said assertively.

"Ok Patti, take out all the ingredients from the pantry. The pressure cooker is in the cupboard below the microwave, but I beg ya make me a cup of tea first."

I swing into action washing my hands and pull our cups out of the cupboard. I pause briefly at the fridge door to study all the small photos of the children Veronica fostered after me. Some stayed with us for respite care for a few days. Others came in the middle of the night for emergency care. One or two were placed with us for weeks and months and others for years. All had their photo taken by Veronica and placed on the fridge doors and the fridge was littered with them.

Every day is Christmas day Veronica had said to me once. These children are moved so frequently between 0 and 18, they often missed Christmas day with their own families. So, our home had a Christmas tree up with lights and decorations the whole year round. Presents, which were gender specific, were wrapped under the tree. Every child leaving her care left with a Christmas gift to enjoy and treasure from Veronica.

She insisted that all the children called her by her first name. She said that them calling her mum was not appropriate 'because they all has mother's.' Calling her Auntie, especially for the younger ones would be adding to the confusion because they were not blood-related, Mrs Scotland was too formal, so Veronica was applicable. So, for the first 17 years of being placed with Veronica, I called her by her first name too. It took a big leap to start calling her Mum. I used to wonder why she didn't adopt me sooner, but she explained back then it was difficult for her to be able to even foster children as a single black woman. Social services did not make it easy, as she did not fit the criteria. She had to prove herself by becoming a registered childminder first and working her way up from there. At the time of my placement, there was a campaign to place black children with black foster parents and she was the only black person in their fostering database. I didn't even have a name when I arrived and hence she named me.

After we finished our teas, I brought out a canister filled with split peas, sweet potatoes and white Irish potatoes, carrots, yams, onions, spinach. Whilst we peeled and prepped the vegetables, I told Veronica about Marcus' dad passing,

"Cudear," she said sympathetically, "poor Marcus, pass on my condolences to he and de family and de rest..." she drifted off the subject, "Patti, see if that lamb defrosted for me, if so, wash it and de pigtails and drop dem in the pressure cooker for me with the peas."

I shuffled to the sink in Veronica's spare slippers and obediently followed her instructions, thankfully the neck of lamb had defrosted and was already cut into pieces. One less job to do. I returned to the table to carry on peeling the carrots. I could see Yolanda all cosy on the sofa with her books studying. She wasn't going to give her grandmother any reasons for permitting her from going to Jamaica with me. The pressure cooker was hissing in the background filling the kitchen with the aroma that was so familiar to me when I was a child. I hated soup back then. I hated anything foreign.

"Why can't we have normal food like my friends at school?" I complained.

Veronica made all her meals from scratch and she only cooked in one pot. Either you ate what she made, or you went without. When the hunger pangs hit you, you ate up everything including cou-cou and saltfish. Now I didn't mind eating the national dish of Barbados once in a while, but eating slimy okras was a challenge for some adults let alone children.

There was no point striking up a conversation as the old pressure cooker was in full swing and the hissing was no longer background noise. I knew it would be over in about 10 minutes and the meat would be ready for the next stage, I went back to the larder unit to look for the ingredients to make the dumplings. Bajans add sugar to their dumplings and it's the best bit of Veronica's soup. The more dumplings the better as far as I'm concerned. I have tried to replicate this element of the soup several times, but my dumplings always fall apart in the pot, so I watch Veronica closely. I suspect I added too much cornmeal the last time.

Veronica at the stove now transfers the meat and peas to a large pot. She washes the veg and adds all except for the spinach, which I know she will add to the pot right at the end before serving. She adds a sachet of Grace Cock soup-mix and a little more water then covers the pot, reducing the heat so the soup can simmer. Once the soup starts to boil, Veronica adds the dumplings in a clockwise direction starting at the edge and working towards the centre of the pot. This ensures the dumplings don't stick together.

Veronica sits back down at the table, "Food's nearly done Yolanda, put down the book and go and wash your hands," she orders.

"Yes, Nan I'm starving man!" Yolanda responds.

"That child of mine is always hungry!" I say annoyed.

"Let the girl be Patti, she's as skinny as a rake she needs building up!" Veronica surmises.

Yolanda joins us at the table, "Nan is there anything I can do?"

Veronica and I look at each other and burst out laughing.

I enjoy every morsel of the soup appreciating the sweetness of the dumplings and the saltiness of the pigtails. Veronica and Yolanda have empty bowls too. Yolanda rinses the bowls and the other cutlery and places them in the dishwasher. We retire to the living room and relax before 'X Factor' comes on. I can feel fatigue kicking in and I start dozing in the armchair. I think Veronica is asleep.

"Mum remember you need to speak to Nan. The holiday?"

"Yes," I said quickly trying to hush Yolanda up.

"What holiday?" Veronica asks abruptly. "What's going on?" she said raising her voice and sitting bolt upright in her chair.

"You might as well tell her Yolanda," I say nervously abdicating responsibility to my daughter.

"Well, you know Marcus' dad died yeah?" explained Yolanda.

"Yeah," her Nan replied.

"And you know the funeral's in Jamaica yeah?"

"Yeah," her Nan confirmed.

"Marcus bought us two tickets to Jamaica and we're flying out to Jamaica next week!" Yolanda exclaimed, "Fantastic isn't it?"

The silence was deafening so deafening even the contestants on the X Factor had gone mute. Yolanda sensing the tension in the air asked her Nan if she was alright. Veronica claimed her headache had returned worse than before and we needed to call an ambulance.

As Yolanda hurried to grab her mobile phone, I watched Veronica hold her head in her hands.

"Looka mi Crosses doh na!" She exclaimed.

"Try not to worry Nan; I'm going to call an ambulance for you now!" Yolanda said tearfully.

"Don't call the ambulance for me child, I'll be fine, call the ambulance for you mudda because I'm about to give she the lashes she should have gotten when she was a child!"

14 ~ CHARMAINE

The good thing about getting up so early in Jamaica is I get the chance to think clearly for the first time in years. I have been going for long walks on the beach in the mornings and spending time with Medina in the afternoon learning how to cook Jamaican food. At night whilst Junior is out and about with the locals, I lie down and reflect on my life. My Dad passing away as a result of a car accident still upsets me to this day, he was working two jobs to keep a roof over our heads, and he fell asleep at the wheel of the car. We were told that he died instantly. I was fourteen years old and that was when I spiralled out of control. My Mum tried her best to control me, but she was grieving for her husband too. They were childhood sweethearts having met at secondary school in Kingston. They were married for years before I unexpectedly came along and whilst they both loved me, my father adored me. I was a Daddy's girl. My Mum only really showed interest in me after my Dad died, but it was too late. I began bunking off school and hanging out with my girlfriends, which was nothing major but at the weekends I was on the missing list from Friday lunchtime until Monday morning and my poor Mum had no idea where I was. She must have been worried sick! My 'friends' and I were not just happy to go out raving we were in for the long haul which included attending the after parties at seedy dances and 'sheebeens'. A typical night out for us would start at Monique's house smoking weed before going to a dancehall reggae concert at The Rex (our favourite East London music venue) wearing the tightest outfits, we could squeeze ourselves into. We would just about have enough money to get in, so that meant we had to cadge drinks from some guys once we got inside and that was very easy to do because we were the loudest, we knew all the slackest dance moves in the place and we drew a lot of attention from the lads. At some point during the night, someone would suggest going on to another club or dance and as long as we were driven there and there was a supply of alcohol or weed, my crew and me would roll with that.

Reflecting back, I shudder when I think of all the risks we took back then, going off with strangers when we were all fuelled with substances, was never a bright idea. It was on one of these typical nights that I met Junior at The Rex. He'd been performing songs from his brand-new album. In the middle of the set, he invited four girls from the crowd to represent their 'endz' in an impromptu dancing competition. I went up on stage to represent East London and the slacker the lyrics, the dirtier I danced on stage and I only went and won the competition, the prize being a meet and greet session with Junior 'Sweetboy' Manley.

After the concert, my crew and I went backstage. After we took photos and got a CD, he whispered in my ear to dump my mampy friends and come out with him on a date. I dumped them in a heartbeat and went with him and his friends to somewhere in Harlesden. The basement flat was a complete dive, the kind of place where you wipe your feet off on the way out and you could count the women, on one hand, the place full of pure roadman. I think I was only protected because I was with Junior and I have to admit I was excited by it all. Junior knew everybody and everybody knew him, he was bump fisting everybody as he walked through to the sound system turning occasionally to make sure I was alright. I swear one of the women bounced into me on purpose but Junior quickly defused the situation, good job he did because I would have taken my earrings out and gone ape on her and dragged the dusty extensions from her head. At some point during the night, Junior got me a drink, he pushed me against the wall, and we danced until the sun came up. He finally dropped me home at 12 noon. I doubt he even looked back to see if I got inside safely but I was delighted when he called later to take me out again.

I felt so grown up in comparison to my friends, but again on reflection, they were never proper dates. Junior always had his boys hanging around him, whenever he wanted to say something private to me he had to whisper it in my ear and the closest we ever got to a date was Junior asking me if I wanted a patty or chicken and chips. I cannot believe my standards and expectations were so low. I was a very cheap date; feed me, give me a spliff or a bottle of Canei and I was happy for him to call me his girl. I always suspected even way back then that there were other girls, but I was his number one chick as he introduced me to his associates as 'wifey'.

Whenever I turned up somewhere with Junior, some dirty sket would try to dance up with him like I wasn't there with him but given the choice he always chose me. The next eighteen months went on in a similar vein until one day he asked me out of the blue if I was pregnant. I asked him why and he said because I had put on a lot of weight recently. I tried to think back and check the dates, but I honestly could not remember when I last had a period, so Junior took me to the supermarket and bought me a digital pregnancy testing kit. When he heard me crying in the loo when we got back to his friend's flat it was obvious to even Stevie Wonder that I was with child.

When Junior said, "don't cry we'll get married." I cried even harder.

Now I am lying here alone in Jamaica trying to stay cool in one of the spare bedrooms. I have no idea where Junior is and neither do I care. He'll make his way home eventually stinking of weed and alcohol. I can hear the fan whirling away in the darkness, but a fat lot of good that's doing for me, all its doing is pushing the warm air around the room. I could open the window and pray the mosquitoes don't make it through the screens and the net which is strategically high around the queen size bed, however, the mosquitoes have already feasted on me during the day and I don't think I could handle any more of their vicious bites. I have tried sprays, lotions, potions and I even dabbed Wray & his Nephew on my skin. Medina burns citronella coils in the house but somehow one of the bitches and her family got in and bit me and now I look like I have two elbows on my left arm. Apparently, they are clever mosquitoes too and have learned to hide under the bed to avoid the poisonous sprays.

I take a cool shower in an attempt to cool down, but as soon as I put my nightie on beads of sweat appear on my body and I'm hot all over again. If I take off my nightie and sleep in the nude, Junior will think it's an invitation for him to resume his conjugal rights and nothing a gwarn like that anymore; he can get his kicks somewhere else for all I care. I turn my face to the pillow, and I start to sob. I miss my Dad; I miss my Mum and I miss my children terribly. Wait! Who is crying…?

15 ~ ROSE

When we get back from the chapel of rest the house is packed with our neighbours and friends coming to offer condolences to the family, to commiserate and to celebrate the life of the late Overseer, Carlos Morgan. Traditionally nine nights is the coming together of the community of friends and family over nine nights of prayer and singing hymns. Mother Morgan had agreed to one night of celebrations as the funeral was coming up, and the Homegoing Celebration for her husband's church family in Kingston Jamaica. I have never seen so much Jamaican cuisine in one place. Courtesy of our neighbours the kitchen is packed with trays and bowls of ackee and saltfish, callaloo, steam mackerel, dumplings, escovitch fish, plantain, boiled yam & cassava, sweet potato pone, rice and peas, jerk pork chops and baked chicken with all of the heavenly aromas hitting my senses at one time.

I avoid Manley like the plague although I am acutely aware of what my punishment will be later. Until then I busy myself in the kitchen trying to make myself useful to Medina and Mother Morgan and they both appreciate my help. After another lengthy prayer by Manley, I fix the table with plates and cutlery. I make a big show of fixing Manley an elaborate plate of food to eat, to the satisfaction of the women present; I smile all animated as I serve him with his favourite foods. This, of course, is all a show and Manley smiles back telling the menfolk at the table that he is blessed with such a beautiful and thoughtful wife who can cook. When he raises his hand, I dutifully placed a knife and fork in it. Charmaine is watching me like I have gone completely mad. She is standing at the kitchen island tucking into her plate rolling her eyes. I guess Junior will have to look after himself or starve. I make up Esther's formula milk and find a plastic jug to cool the bottle down. Esther is comfortable laying in her grandmother's arms enjoying being the centre of attention and smiling at people who are ultimately strangers to her. I believe she has the sixth sense to be aware that she is amongst her family and she was feeling the love. I fix a small plate for Mother Morgan and placed it on a tray, which I put on the coffee table in the adjoining sitting room, and I take Esther from her so she could eat.

Marcus starts the storytelling at the table he is

recalling the story of when one of the brothers had broken a crystal glass in Mother Morgan's cabinet. None of the brothers would admit to their father which one of them had dared to remove the glass and which one of them was the culprit who broke it, which meant all three boys got lashes with the belt from their father. Marcus finally admits now his dad had passed away he wanted to confess before friends and family, that it was he who committed the deadly sin of smashing the glass when he was playing football in the front room. Everybody laughs. Even Mother Morgan chuckles and feigns being upset in between chewing her curried goat and rice.

Manley recalls his father coming down to school when one of his teachers refused to let him sit an exam in computer science and how articulate his dad was when reasoning with the head of computer science and the headmaster. To Manley's delight not only did he sit the exam, he passed his 'O' level with a grade A. The headmaster duly invited his dad to become a parent governor at the school, one of the first Afro Caribbean parent governors in South London. Mother Morgan bursts with pride at the memory and she opens the first of many hymns, 'Abide with Me.'

Seeing that Junior was struggling to find something

nice to say and with everybody picking up on the tension, Mother Morgan leads a second hymn, 'It is Well with My Soul.' Afterwards Junior speaks, "I didn't really know my father until I went up to foreign, but my old man worked really hard for his family all his life. There was always food in the cupboards and drinks in the fridge. The light and gas was always on and my brothers and I had decent clothes to wear. I just wish I'd told him thank you, whilst he was still here to hear it." Raising his half-empty glass of what looked like Guinness punch he said, "To my namesake, my hero, Overseer Carlos Morgan may he eternally rest in peace."

There was a long pause with everybody lost in thought, pensively thinking about his or her own mortality. What followed was a series of neighbours telling their stories and memories of Overseer Morgan then more hymns and more eating and drinking. Some people left and other people arrived, and the storytelling continued into the early hours of the morning, which suited me fine as I dreaded going into the bedroom and being alone with Manley.

Much later when the majority of the crowd had left, and the dominos came out Mother Morgan retired to her bedroom calling me to come into her bedroom with her and close the door behind me. That phrase and 'close the door behind you' conjured up 100 Memories from my childhood and teenage years. Close the door behind you meant I have something very important to tell you for your ears only, close the door behind you meant, come into my sanctuary and I'm going to tell you all my secrets and wisdom. Wisdom about motherhood, sisterhood and being a woman and what I may have to tell you is not going to be pretty either way. I was dreading what Mother Morgan may have to say to me.

"Sister Rose, what happened between you and Manley when we were out? He appeared to be ever so cross with you, is everything okay?"

I wanted to tell her, "No actually everything isn't Okay, your son rapes me, your son really doesn't love me the way I should be loved, your son rules the house with an iron fist and I'm certain that the girls are afraid of him. We're in debt up to our eyeballs because your son gambles away any money that comes into our orbit and he's obsessed with having another child and to keep on having children until I give him a boy!"

I tell her none of this as it would be disloyal to Manley. Furthermore, he is the apple of his mother's eye, following a generation of pastors, elders and deacons.

The Morgan family are like the royal family of church ministers across Jamaica. No, I wouldn't dare say a word; I decide to just play the game until I work out my next move. I put on my biggest smile and reply,

"All is well."

I feel like a lamb, to the slaughter, I leave her bedroom and lay on the bed obediently waiting for my husband.

16 ~ PATTI

F acebook has an app called, 'On This Day.' and it shows you exactly what you posted on this day back in 2015, 2014, 2013... right back until the first year, you joined. On this day back in 2014, I checked myself in at Probation HQ in Victoria. I think I was on a training course and I must have been inspired because I went on to post loads of motivational and uplifting posts later that day. If I remember rightly, the training event was pitched at middle managers about our responsibilities for safeguarding children and our duty to share information with other statutory organisations to protect vulnerable children. I was so fired up by the end of the day I went home and wrote a workshop for my team on how to conduct home visits. When I finally delivered the training event with the Practice Development Officer, this particular workshop was well received by the practitioners working in our cluster.

What a difference a couple of years make, as on this day, this year, I am checking myself in on Facebook into a five-star all-inclusive hotel in Negril Jamaica. In fact, we arrived in Jamaica last night. Marcus met Yolanda and I at Sangster International Airport, Montego Bay and when we arrived at the Cliff Hotel, we were both overwhelmed by how beautiful everything was. Our luggage was taken by the porter who we followed into the plush hotel lobby to join the queue of tourists who were trying the check-in, having just arrived at the hotel on the transfer coach. Marcus had a word with a passing member of staff then we were immediately taken out of the queue, taken to a private area of the main lobby and seated in deep welcoming comfy armchairs. I could see that a few of the other weary travellers were wondering why we were given preferential treatment and so were my daughter and I. Then the next minute we were given warm flannels to wipe our hands and incredibly large glasses of Rum Punch. One sip told me instantly that the punch was made with Wray & Nephew Overproof rum, it warmed up my mouth and throat as it travelled down to my tummy. I set the glass aside and asked for some ice water and before I could blink the waitress came back with a jug of ice water and a tall glass and set it on the desk in front of us. In the meantime, while Yolanda and I sipped our drinks and looked around, Marcus continued to liaise with the concierge, confirming his name, address, email address etc. I overheard him telling her his membership number and her advising him how many points he had accumulated from his previous visit. Yolanda and I could not contain our excitement at being in a plush location and to top it all we saw a couple in their wedding attire who had obviously just got married at the hotel as they passed us to take photos at the front of the hotel. The bride looked beautiful in a halter neck white gown; she was being pushed in her wheelchair by her handsome husband who was also dressed in white. They were beaming from ear to ear, clearly happy to be starting a life together as man and wife.

"Welcome home Mr Morgan and welcome to Jamaica to your wife and Daughter," said the receptionist. "Can I put on your wristbands please?"

We all readily complied with her request and then she informed us of the fact that as members our rooms were upgraded to Junior Suites with resort and ocean views plus a late check-out time, which meant we could make use of the room until an hour before we were due to leave in two weeks' time. Yolanda and I were amazed and by the time we finally saw our rooms we were speechless. Yolanda jumped straight onto her bed screaming. Mine and Marcus' suite was equally as nice, but right now all I wanted to do was shower, change and eat dinner before the restaurant closed for the evening. I told Yolanda to be ready and by the lift in 15 minutes. I needn't have worried about missing dinner as the main restaurant was still in full swing by the time we got downstairs, in fact, we had to wait a further 20 minutes to be seated. I scanned the dining area to make sure we were dressed appropriately; again, I needn't have worried because, in my opinion, we were overdressed.

Given the blisteringly hot weather, when presented with the option of dining inside or alfresco, we chose to eat outside. I could hear the waves crashing in, reminding me that the beach was not very far away, and I made a mental note of making sure I got up with enough time to take a sea bath in the morning just like I did when I went to Barbados. My Mum insisted we take a sea bath every morning, even though there was a perfectly good pool on the Hotel complex where we were staying in beautiful St James. Mum pointed out the many benefits of having a sea bath both physically and spiritually and it was something I intended to continue on this holiday too.

The menu at this restaurant was extensive with so much choice with cuisine from all over the world, and everything was delicious. After dinner, we took a leisurely stroll through the hotel to enjoy the evening's entertainment and we were seated with another family who I soon found out were a week into their two-week vacation. Very soon, Marcus struck up a conversation with the husband Tim, and it was not long until they were drinking Red Stripes like they were old friends. Yolanda and his daughters, Lasonta and Fawn bonded like long lost sisters and they were swiftly off to check out the band at the front of the stage. I moved my chair closer to have a chat with Tim's wife Genetha, who reassured me that the resort was a safe place and the girls would be fine. I gathered that the resident band this week was called Tranzishan, originally from Barbados, who were touring the Caribbean. As I sipped my drink and listened to them play, I was impressed that although they were all teenagers, they were very talented. I loved their unique blend of reggae and jazz and I really wanted to get up and 'cut the rug' with Marcus, but I found it difficult to keep my eyes open. I kept them open long enough to see Yolanda and the girls gyrating on the dance floor and giggling at the band members, even from where I was sitting I could see the boys were hot looking, especially the drummer! Marcus could see that I was getting tired and excused himself from his new buddy; we said goodnight and made our way back to our room. Tim and Genetha told us that they would look out for Yolanda and would make sure that they escorted her back to her room later.

Over the years, I had heard a lot about Jamaica both good and bad and I was super excited about finally venturing there until I told Mum, who instead of being happy for me proceeded to tell me one hundred and one horror stories about Jamaica with each one getting worse as she went on. We both knew the real reasons why she was not happy, a) I was not going to her beloved Barbados, b) Her nose was put out of joint because she had not yet met Marcus and Antoinette had, and c) I was taking Yolanda out of college when she had exams the following Spring. In my opinion, the latter point was the only valid one. But I argued that Yolanda had her head in a book most of the time and she could benefit from a short break. At least Bev at work was excited for me, saying that Negril was a beautiful place and there was lots to see and do there. I doubted we were going to get to visit all those places, but I definitely wanted to climb Dunn's River Falls in Ocho Rios in the north of the island. I hoped I could make the climb without falling and bussing my backside. Marcus laughed out loud when I told him that one and promised he would never let go of my hand.

Well, my first night in Jamaica was spent with my legs wrapped around Marcus' back and this morning I am sitting on the balcony on the sixth floor overlooking an amazing resort with my mobile phone automatically connecting to the Wi-Fi and updating my social networking accounts. Marcus is making me a cup of Blue Mountain coffee, he knows I am not a coffee drinker, but he promises me that Jamaican coffee is the bomb. All I know is the aroma is intoxicating and I am looking forward to trying it more than I am looking forward to meeting Marcus' family. Marcus' dad's Homegoing Celebration is in five days' time and that is the real reason we are here in the first place. I have bought a gift for his mum and I hope she likes it. Marcus brings me my coffee and we chill on the patio whilst I update my Facebook profile to read 'PATTI SCOTLAND IS IN A

RELATIONSHIP WITH MARCUS MORGAN' on my phone. By the time Yolanda calls, we are ready to go downstairs for breakfast.

17 ~ CHARMAINE

I am sure I hear someone crying and it doesn't sound like Mother Morgan to me! My money is on Rose, something happened at that Jerk Hut because Manley looked proper vex, so much so he could not contain himself. Rose was making excuses for him saying it had been a long day and Manley was stressed. Stressed my ass we're all stressed! Pop's funeral is in the morning, but I guess Manley is fallible like everybody else after all. Bloody punk! I must have drifted off, 'cause Junior is asleep beside me and I wonder how he can sleep so peacefully beside me. He looks like a cherub without a care in the world. I wonder what he dreams about 'cause every time I close my eyes I think about his affairs, the fights the twins witnessed and the court case when he humiliated me.

I clearly remember the very first time he hit me. Yes, there were many threats quite early on in our relationship but he never followed through and he never hit me during my pregnancy, but Junior went on a bender with his friends when the twins were about 12 weeks old, I remember because I was still breastfeeding and was absolutely exhausted. He came home at about two in the morning beating down the door as he had forgot his door keys. I threw them down to him out of the window telling him to keep his voice down as the babies were sleeping. He came crashing up the stairs in a right state, waking up the twins. I pushed past him to get to the babies Moses basket and I managed to settle Gaby, but Gary was ready for another feed. I settled back on the bed to begin nursing him and I was cussing Junior off for not helping me with the children that, he wanted to keep. Junior lets me know that his mother raised three children on her own when his father was away working on the mission field on another Caribbean island.

Now I blame myself for what happened next as I proceeded to tell him to, "fuck yu mudda!" Why I disrespected his mother, I don't know. Mother Morgan has always been nice to me when I have spoken to her on the phone, but there is no excuse for what Junior did next. He turned towards me in the bed and chucked me a box clean in my face. I never saw it coming and I didn't have a chance to protect myself because I was holding

Gary in my hands. I was dizzy momentarily, Junior took Gary from me and I used the baby's blanket to stem the flow of the bleeding and in that instant, I knew I should have told him to, "eff off and leave!" or called the police but I did not because I was ashamed and I felt that I deserved it. I saw the panic in his eyes, he was expecting some kind of reaction, but I was too shocked to react. Had I thrown him out way back then I would have been sparing myself another four years of violence, betrayal and heartache.

In the following years Junior and I have fought like banned dogs at an illegal dog fight, some of the fights he has instigated and some I have started because I suspected he was cheating on me and despite his protests, I was proven right when he gave me an STI. Not even my Mum knows, that I may find it difficult to have more children because I contracted Chlamydia from him.

Before I smother Junior in his sleep, I decide to get out of bed. When I rise, I see fresh mosquito bites on my arms and legs and all I do is kiss my teeth. I pull on my sports bra, a T-shirt and a pair of running shorts and I head straight out on to the verandah, only pausing to say, "Good Morning." to Medina, who is already awake making breakfast. I am surprised that it is already warming up and bright with the locals out and about at 5 o'clock in the morning.

I begin by doing some stretches that Dave my personal trainer taught me in West Ham Park. I use the term 'personal trainer' loosely. I was out jogging in the park when I came across a group of women who were working out with this guy and he wasn't ramping with them at all. I asked if I could join in, since then I've been working out with him and the Golden Girls for the past few weeks. What I like about Dave is that he is not just concerned about exercise, but he also addresses your diet as well. I was comfort eating on a lot of shit. Dave stresses that warming up before exercise and cooling down properly after our runs is as important as the workout itself, and most important is eating clean, which is so much easier to achieve here in Jamaica. In fact, it's probably the first time I have eaten clean in my entire adult life. Medina cooks every meal here from scratch, with the freshest ingredients available and I love it all. There's always fresh fruit to make smoothies and I'm loving Callaloo with my evening meals. I have been able to stick to eating chicken or fish and Medina makes the best fruit juices with mangoes and pineapples from the kitchen garden. I make a mental note saying that is exactly what I'm going to have for breakfast after my run this morning and then I'll fill my boots on the hard food as today is going to be a long day.

When I look around the tiny cul-de-sac and admire the pretty bungalows, peeping out through the greenery and I experience the lifestyle here in Jamaica, all I can think is, "fuck wanting to live in Wanstead." Negril is the place to be; right on this road. It's fucking beautiful. There are about 12 houses on this cul-de-sac with a large roundabout in the middle and the residents have utilised the space for their kitchen garden. Personally, I can't tell one plant from the next, but Mother Morgan told me there is squash, tomatoes, callaloo, runner beans and sweet potatoes growing, and thriving over there. I love the community spirit here. Everybody knows each other and there hasn't been an evening since Pops Morgan died that a neighbour hasn't popped in to see us bearing gifts of cooked food, fruits and expressions of condolence. Miss Brown at the first bungalow on the corner can bake! Shit! I had one of her currant slices and I had to go for a night run to work off the calories, and Miss Grant who lives opposite came over with a tray full of homemade coconut drops and gizzadas, I'm not a fan of coconut but I ate the pastry off the gizzada and gave the filling to Junior. Miss Clarke who is the next-door neighbour to our left, made jerk chicken and jerk pork last night, don't tell my Mum but the chicken tasted really good. So good, I happily chewed on the bone! I catch a glimpse out of the corner of my eye, I see someone watching me from one of the loungers on the verandah and I realise it's Marcus.

"Fuck me, Marcus!" I said clutching my chest, "You almost gave me a heart attack!"

"Sorry Charmaine," he replies sadly, "go ahead and do your thing."

"OK, wanna join me for a run?" I ask.

"Yeah, you sure you can keep up with me?"

"I'll try," I answer.

Marcus gets up and stretches, he puts on his T-shirt and I avert my eyes as he does so. He joins me for my final stretches and then I follow him down the steps. We jog in a clockwise direction around the roundabout down to the main road called Norman Manley Boulevard.

As we pass our neighbours they all shout, "Good Morning." and we duly reply.

That's another thing I like about Jamaica everybody is polite and I believe the twins would thrive in a community like this and I would gladly follow Junior out here if he wasn't so hell-bent on staying in the UK. The sun is very hot today, only Jah knows how hot it's going to get later on in the day. Marcus grabs my arm to cross the main road and he hails an old Rastaman setting up his stall at the side of the road, with what looks like a mountain of coconuts that he's preparing for the passing trade.

He warmly yells back, "Yes Boss, check me when you're going back up, seen?"

Coral Beach is virtually empty, I can see an elderly couple enjoying their sea bath and we greet them as we jog by. Jogging on the sand is a new experience but I manage to keep up with Marcus and I am impressed with myself. We pass some awesome looking beach condos and I can see the beach resort appearing in the distance. Not before long, I am sweating like a pig and panting away, so we sit on the beach and watch the fishermen getting ready to go out to sea to catch the fish of the day. I love listening to their banter and laughter even though I can't make out what they are saying. They remind me of Junior and his brethren when they used to come over to the house to play dominoes. It was one of the few times you'd catch

Junior in the kitchen making Ital soup or Oxtail. I signal to Marcus that break time is over and we continue to jog up past the Coconut International Restaurant, onto Bourbon Beach until we get to the Sandals Negril Beach Resort & Spa. Wow! Next time I come to Jamaica I must stay here. Somehow, we manage to jog back to the public entrance of Coral Beach and Marcus asks if I want a drink and all I can do is nod because I'm trying to catch my breath. We head for the Ras, who smiles when he sees us and it's a wide toothless grin.

"Good Morning Massa Morgan!" He says so formally.

"Morning Ras," Marcus replies.

"And Good Morning, Fluffy Diva!" The Ras addresses me, and I greet him back.

Marcus says, "Gimme two a de coconut dere Ras!"

The Ras picks up a coconut still in its casing and expertly uses the cutlass to chop off the head of the coconut to create a small hole in the top and he passes the first coconut to Marcus who then passes it to me. In no time, the Ras is passing the second freshly prepared coconut to Marcus. I watch as Marcus puts the coconut straight to his mouth and starts to drink and I think to myself, "I'm not doing that." Seeing the scornful look on my face, Marcus grabs a straw out of a little box on the cart and inserts it into the coconut. I take a few sips and even though it is refreshing, as I said before, I really don't like the taste of coconut so when Marcus has finished his, I give him mine and he drinks that too. I notice the Ras is smiling away studying me.

He says to Marcus, "Your wife nuh like the coconut water?"

And without missing a beat Marcus replies, "She's my sister in law, Junior's beautiful wife."

"Oh-oh-oh! I heard Junior went up to foreign and married an English gyal and now I finally get to meet her!" Turning to me he went on to ask me directly, "So, Fluffy Diva, isjustdetwopickneyahave?"

"Sorry, what did you say?" I ask.

"I said; is it just the two pickney that you have?" He replied deliberately slowing his words down.

"Oh, Yes I have twins, a boy and a girl," I say proudly.

"Blessings!" he responds, "If you were my ooman, you would be pregnant all de time." Then he cackles with laughter.

Me with my feisty self, respond by saying, "Ras, you can't handle this Fluffy Diva you know."

As I turn to cross the road he says, "Don't let the grey hair fool you; there may be snow on the mountain top but there's fire in de Valley!"

I cut my eye after him and cross the road and wait for Marcus.

The Ras gives him something and shouts loud enough for me to hear, "Marcus, put some of this on her skin, dem dutty mosquitoes dun messed up her pretty red skin!"

When Marcus catches up with me, I'm already halfway up the road and I can see Junior sitting on the verandah. Marcus catches up to me apologising for the Ras' behaviour, he advises me to apply the aloe vera sap on my skin, and it should help to bring the swelling down on my mosquito bites.

"So, where have you been with my wife," Junior says accusingly as we approach the house.
"I notice you and her are like batty and bench these days!"

I can tell Junior is spoiling for a fight, so I don't answer but go inside and stand behind the mosquito screen so I can see what happens next.

"Well I'm surprised you remembered she's your wife, you've hardly spent any time with her since we got here,"

Marcus says angrily as he steps towards Junior, "…and don't you worry about me and Charmaine, my Empress is already here in Jamaica you'll see her on Saturday at the Homegoing Celebration!" Marcus screams to a shocked Junior but my heart stops at the revelation.

"Bruv, you got a woman? I was beginning to wonder if you were a batty boy!" Laughed Junior.

With two giant steps, Marcus closes in on Junior and grabs him by the throat shouting, "We're burying our Dad today, one more bloodclaart word and I'll be burying you beside him, tu raas!"

Hearing the noise, Manley pushes past me, and he manages to break them up. Seeing it's all over, I go back into the bedroom pick up my shower bag and towel and head for the bathroom. Trust Manley to spoil all the fun.

18 ~ROSE

"Scream one more time Rose!" Manley spits coldly as he thumps me in my stomach. "Wake up this baby or my family and I'll wake up some blows in your deceitful skin." He says as he thumps me in my stomach several more times. I try to curl up on the bed to protect my head and stomach, but he is still able to find a spot to punch me where it hurts the most. I cry silent tears knowing it will get worse for me if I try to talk or reason with him when he is so angry. As far as Manley is concerned, I have disobeyed him, and I need to be punished. He threw my tablets away in the bin at the Jerk Hut and told me that we were going to try for another baby when we got indoors. He stops punching me and forces himself on me. I cry throughout the whole ordeal and afterwards, he turns away, moves as far from me as he can on his parent's big bed, and shuns me as though I am a leper and he falls asleep.

When I am confident that he is in a deep sleep I put my dressing gown on and look through my suitcase for my spare medication, thank goodness Dr Oko had given me so much of it. After finding my tablets, I slip out of the door to the kitchen to get a glass of water. Fortunately, the light is still on and I manage to find where the glasses are kept. The thing about having staff in the home is that they never let you go in the kitchen; it was Medina's domain and she gets so offended if you say you can help yourself. The whole thing about having helpers and kitchen staff is not something that I am accustomed to and it does not sit well with me either, but I suppose it provides local employment and Mother Morgan with company in the house, now Pops is gone. I place the cold glass on my stomach hoping the cold ice will somehow soothe away all the pain, but it offers no ease. Manley knew what he was doing when he beat me in that area as the chances of anybody seeing bruising in my midriff is slim to nil; even if I was wearing a swimsuit.

Medina startles me when she appears from the darkness of the servant's quarters. She acknowledges me but she doesn't say a word. She fills the kettle at the sink, and it hisses into action when she plugs it in. She shuffles around the kitchen finding two cups and makes a fresh pot of tea. She gives me a cup and sits opposite me and drinks her tea, which is still steaming hot. I can tell from the smell that she'd made bush herbal tea from Cerasee, it smells awful. My Mum used to boil it for me to drink when I had cramps during my menstrual cycle, and it didn't matter how much milk, honey or sugar you added the tea always tasted so bitter. Somehow knowing she had made the tea to help me feel better made me cry. Again, she did not speak but left a note on the table with the Bible scripture 2 Timothy Chapter 3 verses 1-8. After I finish drinking the tea, Medina washes up our cups and turns them upside down on the draining board. I say thank you and go back to my room to look up the verses the old lady gave me.

Almost 12 hours later I am lying in bed alone, feeling exhausted and experiencing pain all over my body. I am reflecting on everything that happened at the funeral today. Everybody says that funerals are an all-day affair and they are right, but paradoxically, the day can also pass very quickly, so I am here to let you know what went down.

First of all, Marcus and Junior had a fight on the veranda first thing in the morning and when Manley heard the commotion he had to push pass Charmaine to part them. I do not understand why Charmaine stood up there like a statue and she did not say a word, it's almost like she wanted Marcus to beat up her husband and when Manley did intervene, she simply turned and went into her bedroom. Fortunately, the all-seeing Medina turned up the radio so Mother Morgan could not hear what was going on, as it would have been very distressing for her to hear her children fighting. When the brothers came inside it was in time to hear the announcements of the newly departed on the radio and the details of their father's funeral. They froze to listen and the reality of it all appeared to knock some sense back into them as I could see the tension dissipate amongst them. Manley looked sternly at them calling for a truce and they agreed with a couple of nods and things were back to normal…whatever normal is.

Thereafter, it was all panic stations with everybody trying to bathe and get ready at the same time. I was intending to wear a black linen dress with a black jacket that I normally wear to funerals during the summer months in the UK. Unfortunately for me, being a nursing mother, I could not breastfeed Esther in that outfit, so I wore a black skirt with a crisp white shirt with a black jacket. When I joined the family on the verandah, I noticed straightaway that Charmaine and I were in similar outfits and for some reason I was comforted by that. It was like we were truly bonded as sisters, united in our grief. I recall arriving at the church and seeing the crowds of people both inside and outside of the church. The church was packed with people from all over Jamaica and the Caribbean. Overseer Morgan would have certainly been humbled by the turnout. Manley introduced me to family members who had come across from Kingston to attend their uncle's funeral. As pleased as I was to meet them, I was anxious to get Esther out of the sun into the cooler sanctuary of the church. I made my way up the centre aisle of the church to the front row, which was reserved, for the immediate family only and a few minutes later a frazzled looking Charmaine joined me. She told me she had been trying to get away from some old Rastaman who had been trying to chat foolishness to her.

Despite her saying, "Don't look now!"
I turned my head to see the old Rastaman dressed in white robes with a matching white turban and a red, gold and green scarf across his shoulders, smiling the widest toothless grin that he could manage in Charmaine's direction. Charmaine made up her face into an

expression, which I read as, "I'll tell you later."

The coffin coming into the church was another difficult moment as the boys and their mother filed in behind. It was all very heartbreaking to witness and of course, I followed suit and started to cry. Charmaine had to nudge me at some point, as my name had been called to sing a solo with the choir. Although I knew, I was going to be singing at the funeral I was still shocked that we were at that part of the service already. I gave Esther to Charmaine and I made my way up to the pulpit and I took the microphone from Bishop Francis who had travelled up from our Kingston branch with his wife to officiate the service. Mother Morgan had requested that I sing Overseer Morgan's favourite song; 'Going up Yonder' by Tramaine Hawkins. As I opened my mouth to sing, I saw Pops Morgan standing by his casket dressed in his chocolate brown suit looking at his wife being comforted by her sons.

His eyes were transfixed on his wife, but he did turn and smile at me during my rendition of his favourite song. I knew if I told anyone within the church circle what I just saw, I would be 'back-benched' from the church. To be back-benched in the Pentecostal movement means that you cannot enjoy the full benefits of being a church member, you are stripped of any position in the church that you hold, you cannot take communion and you have to physically sit at the back of the church.

Years ago, back in the day, I remembered a lovely couple joined our church with their very pretty daughter. She was very much sought after by the brothers in the church, but her parents refused all applications to court her. The parents were so overprotective that she was chauffeur driven all over the place and the only place she was alone was at work. To cut a long story short, the daughter fell pregnant by a colleague she met at work. To her parent's horror, it turns out she was not working overtime after all. Despite the man's intention to marry her as soon as possible the pastor at the time found out and he got fully involved. Not only was their only child thrown out of the choir, but her parents were back-benched as well! It all seemed unfair to me and her parents never recovered from the embarrassment and their treatment by the pastor, the elders and the congregation. Once their suspension was over, they chose to join another denomination altogether and never came back. Their daughter is now a happily married woman, and mother to a daughter but no longer a practising Christian. In my opinion, it's such a shame;

people make mistakes, after all, what about forgiveness, reconciliation and counselling? We have come so far as a church, we even have a Facebook page and a twitter account, but we are still coy about discussing intimacy and sex with our young people. Some Pastors are good about preaching about fornication but say nothing about coping strategies and waiting for marriage.

Manley and I had to find our own way. I will always remember our wedding night with horror. We were treated to a spa weekend in Buckinghamshire; a wedding present from the church. I was so unprepared with no pep talk from my Mother, heck, I hadn't even seen a man naked; not even my Dad! Once in the hotel room, I went to the bathroom to change into my new nightie and sat on the toilet seat thinking about how painful it was going to be losing my virginity to my husband. About forty minutes later Manley knocked the bathroom door and he persuaded me to come out. As tender and gentle as Manley was trying to be, my first sexual experience was painful and over in a few minutes. We were to try again a few times over that weekend, but we never discussed contraception and a few weeks into our marriage, I discovered I was pregnant. I feel short-changed and unfulfilled and the babies came too quickly for me to experiment and work out what I liked and didn't like. It is the same process all the time and sometimes he avoids kissing me altogether, it's the same missionary position every time and he gets upset if I suggest something else or I am not instantly turned on by his prodding and poking. Here in Jamaica, he is even colder towards me and I feel like I am being raped. There I said it, my husband rapes me, and he treats my silence as consent...

Anyway, back to the funeral; the choir was performing at its peak and I was reaching all the high notes and the congregation were standing up, clapping and singing along too. By the time I was finished there wasn't a dry eye in the house. Overseer Morgan waves at me then he disappears. At the graveside, Mother Morgan was so dignified, unlike Junior who had to be restrained by his brothers to prevent him from trying to jump in the grave right on top of the coffin. Back at the church hall, I couldn't count the amount of people who came over to give Esther and I hugs kisses, kind words and condolences. I had a plate of food, but I was interrupted so many times that the food became too cold to eat and I began to feel a little dizzy.

Charmaine was a star, assisting me with Esther;

warming up bottles and changing nappies. The only time I saw her looking tense was when Junior came over to talk to her or when that horrid Rastaman came within her orbit. Only a Jamaican man would flirt with you at a funeral and right under your husband's nose too. I was thinking of rescuing her, but Charmaine looked like she had it all under control. My thoughts were interrupted by a man who introduced himself as Brother Gabriel John.

"Good afternoon Sis Morgan, I am very sorry for your loss," He said in a strong Kingstonian accent. "My sister and I came up from Cherry Gardens last night."

He paused and I replied, "Thank you so much; did you know Overseer Morgan personally?"

"Yes," He replied, "When he attended our church in Kingston, it was a pleasure to hear him preach."

"Oh, Lovely," I said believing that was the end of the conversation.

"I wonder if my sister can speak to you for a few minutes Sis Morgan?"

"Yeah, sure," I replied, and I followed him outside the church into the small cemetery where Pops was buried a few hours ago. Brother Gabriel introduced me to his sister Grace, and I could see the family resemblance straightaway. Sister Grace is a stunningly attractive brown-skinned woman with high cheekbones and small frame wearing a black suit and a huge black brimmed hat. She smiled warmly and received me with open arms, but for some reason, I felt as though I had known her all of my life, as I really felt relaxed in her presence.

"Sis Morgan so very nice to meet you and as my Brother said my name is Grace." She had that very distinctive Kingstonian accent that I love.

"Likewise," I replied, "Thank you for coming all the way from Kingston."

"But I had no choice Sis Morgan, I had to come to pay my respects, but I have to confess that was not my only reason." A knot started to form in my stomach, as she started to explain, "You see Sis Morgan I dreamt of you last night and unfortunately it wasn't a very nice dream at all, at all, at all!" Grace stepped in closer and lowered her voice to ensure she could not be overheard by anyone, "I dreamt you were in a lot of pain at the hands of someone very close to you. The message I have for you is that it's going to get much worse unless you get yourself and your girls away from the situation when you return to the UK." I must have gone very pale because she grabbed me by both hands and said the following, "The Lord is going to send someone to help you and this person will know exactly how to give you the assistance you need. You will meet this person at the Homegoing Celebration. Sis Morgan are you listening to me?"

My mind raced back to the sermon Manley gave at convention; the sermon I helped him to write.

How would she have known about that I ask myself?

"Yes, I heard what you said, and I really appreciate you coming all this way to tell me." I reached into my handbag to retrieve my purse and seeing what I was about to do, Sis Grace softly slaps my hand.

"We're not after your money, Sis Morgan and whatever's in your purse keep on taking them, we're leaving now, God Bless."

I felt my legs almost give way, but I managed to get back inside the church and go straight up to Manley who was talking to Bishop Francis.

"So sorry to interrupt you Hun, but I wanted to thank Bishop for coming up with members of the congregation to support us," and I give him a hug.

"No problem at all but it was agreed that only my wife and I would attend, and the rest of the flock will come down for the Homegoing."

"Bro Gabriel and Sis Grace from your church were

here," I said.

"Who? I don't think I know them,"

"Are you sure?" I questioned him frantically.

"Tell a lie, the last time I saw Overseer Morgan in hospital, he knew he was about to die, and he was talking about his guardian angels Gabriel and Grace... Sis Morgan are you alright?"

I passed out, but before I hit the concrete altar, someone caught me, Medina I think. When I came around, Charmaine was leaning over me trying to cover my bruised stomach with her jacket.

Forgetting where she was she whispered, "What the fuck has Manley been doing to you?"

I closed my eyes, as it was easier to feign fainting rather than tell the truth. I am lying in bed now looking forward to meeting this person at the Homegoing celebration.

19 ~ PATTI

I t has always been on my bucket list to climb Dunn's River Falls and when I tell Marcus he is only too happy to organise a day trip for us starting off with a two-course lunch and a catamaran cruise around the north of the island. We meet our new American friends in the hotel lobby, and we get into an old school bus driven by Lennox, a friend of the family.

We sit up front with Lennox and on our journey from Negril to Ocho Rios, he tells me stories about Marcus' antics when he was a child. Marcus playfully tries to shut him down, but that only makes Lennox embellish his stories even more. Marcus acts as a tour guide pointing out places of interest along the way, from new hotels to the names of flowers and plants that we will never remember. When we get on the highway, Lennox drives at a rate of knots and he's not the only person driving recklessly. The drivers are all driving like madmen, people are joining the motorway any old how and some of the vehicles are clearly not road worthy and would never pass an MOT test in the UK. I am nervous, so I secretly pray to a higher being for the protection and safety of us all. Marcus puts his arm around me, and I feel a little better. Marcus and Lennox don't even bat an eyelid as we're flung about the bus. In fact, I think it brings back memories of childhood going to and from school by school bus, as he starts telling tales of being at secondary school. They sound like good times, but it makes me wonder why his family decided to leave Jamaica in the first place to come to the 'mother country' when they were already living in paradise.

When we arrive at the meeting point, I quickly hop over Marcus, I am the first person to get out of the bus and run over to a nearby bush where I start to vomit. A young man comes over with a bottle of water for me and then he picks a couple of leaves from the bush and sticks them between my locs. The nausea feeling immediately dissipates and I drink the water slowly. I am really grateful, and I thank him. Yolanda ties back my hair and Marcus rubs the small of my back as he gives the young fella some Jamaican dollars.

We then line up and join the line of tourists queuing for lunch. What a spread lunch is, there is macaroni cheese pie, rice and peas, jerk chicken, jerk fish, festivals, hard dough bread and loads of different kinds of salads. I see a tower of fresh fruit consisting of grapes, watermelon, pineapples and the list goes on. There are also copious amounts of rum punch and other alcoholic beverages, but I intend to stick with my water, which is ice cold and refreshing.

After lunch, we all head out to the catamaran and although the temperature is in the high 30s there is a soft breeze coming in from the Caribbean Sea cooling us down nicely. We manage to get seats in the outside part of the boat overlooking the beautiful horizon to the left and the beach and coastline on our right. Tim and Marcus go to the bar to collect our drinks and then we just chill admiring the views and listen to the sweet reggae music playing low over the speakers. I instantly recognise tracks from Bob Marley followed by Beres Hammond and Taurus Riley. I pull down my sun hat to shield my eyes as the catamaran sails off and I really can't remember the last time I was so completely relaxed and happy. That's the right word 'Happy', I glance over at Marcus and he has his phone ready to take a selfie of us together.

"Say cheese, Empress!"

Once at sea, the catamaran comes to a standstill and the crew issue snorkelling equipment to their guests. I can swim but not as confidently as Yolanda who, I discover on this holiday, swims like a fish. Marcus too is an excellent swimmer. I lower myself into the crystal clear water, which is cold at first, but I quickly get used to the temperature. Marcus and Tim take the lead and we all wade in the water and follow them out towards the larger group. The view at the bottom of the sea is amazing, so much to see, including a shipwreck. This ship was purposely sunk at least a decade ago and is now the home to an abundant sea life all living peacefully in amongst each other. We are fortunate to see some turtles swim by and the crew encourages us to throw bread to them. Tim has a waterproof camera and he takes loads of photos of us all having fun. We must have been out here for about 15 minutes, but it feels like it's so much longer. In about another 15 minutes I notice I am almost bone dry again; the sun is that hot.

When we arrive at the falls I notice it's a professional set up on the beach, there are vendors selling waterproof slippers and waterproof cameras, the usual T-shirts and jewellery, which I have seen on sale at the resort. On entering the falls, I notice the lines of tourists and

181

Jamaicans linking hands and snaking up the Dunn's River Falls. It's absolutely crowded with people, adults as well as children. It's reassuring to see the high number of Jamaican guides on the falls who all have royal blue polo shorts on with their names on the back. Then I see a declaration board advising visitors not to climb the falls if they suffer from a range of medical conditions from high blood pressure to heart conditions and I start to get nervous. Not that I suffer from any of those conditions, but I know myself; I can trip up on a flat pavement and there is a serious risk that I could fall and break my neck out here. We are all streamed into lines and fortunately, our little clique stays together, and we are introduced to our guide, Straker. He is a tall dark-skinned man about my age with very rugged features. It is clear that he has worked outside for many years, as his skin looks weathered and glistening. He shouts safety instructions over the noise of the gushing waterfalls.

"Good Afternoon everyone!" he says then turns to Marcus, "and welcome home to Jamaica, Sir," Marcus smiles and acknowledges him back. "Mrs you're first" and he grabs my left hand shouting to the others "Everybody else, link up and join hands behind this beautiful woman! We're going up now!" He shouts. "Mrs, don't worry just put your feet exactly where I put mine."

I look down at his webbed feet for the first time and I am shocked to see he is going to climb up the falls in his bare feet! I climb the falls with the sound of constant encouragement from Straker to place my size 5 ½ feet exactly where he had confidently put his. Yolanda and the girls have long since broken free of our slow line and are making their way up, laughing as they slip and slide against the relentless current of the waterfall. Oh, to be young, confident and carefree like that again, to be able to take risks and not worry about the consequences. There was a time not that long ago that I would have run up these falls and ran all the way back down again. Slowly but surely, I make progress and I even feel confident enough to let go of Straker's hand and jump into the middle of the falls to have my photo taken with Marcus. I am definitely purchasing that photo at the end of this expedition and I cannot wait to show Beverley the photo when I get back to work.

About half an hour later, I am pleasantly surprised when Straker announces that we have reached the top and I see the girls posing under the sign, which reads, 'Congratulations. You have just completed the climb of the World Famous Dunn's River Falls.' I am so proud of myself and at that moment I think, who would have thought that losing my shoe climbing an escalator on the London Underground would lead to me climbing Dunn's River Falls in beautiful Jamaica. Marcus loves me enough to fly me and my daughter here in this beautiful paradise and tomorrow I am going to meet his mother and his family. Am I nervous about meeting them? Hell yes! Who wouldn't be? They only buried their loved one yesterday and they are all still grieving. Also, when Marcus mentioned his brother's behaviour at the funeral I picked up the tension in his voice, making it clear that he wasn't impressed with Junior at all; but attending the Homegoing Celebration and family BBQ was the purpose of my visit and I'd have Yolanda there for moral support. Note to self; I better remember to ring Mummy Veronica to ask her what I should wear to church, as I have not been in years. I usually pray every day though and undertake 10 minutes of meditation first thing in the morning, as many people go to bed at night with dreams, hopes and plans for future and they do not wake up in the morning. Coincidentally though, since I met Marcus I haven't prayed, but he needs my prayers now more than anyone else right about now.

This last week he has split his time between us and

his family. In the middle of the night I have heard him crying, not big belly tears but sobbing, nonetheless. I wanted to go out to him on the balcony to support him, but I know he has chosen that time to be alone and I respect that. He's a proud Jamaican man and I love him. Did I say that out loud? Is it even possible to fall in love with someone after only a few months? I told him and I don't even know if it's reciprocated. I know for sure if I said any of this shit to Ann or Mum they would both queue up to give me a hard lash of reality. The thing is I feel loved and I simply adore him.

It continues to play on my mind back at the hotel. I don't think that I have ever been in love, not even with Yolanda's father and he was in love with his wife. I had a very private fling with a probation officer in south London, but that fizzled out due to the demands of our work. I am 45 years old, in love with a man several years my junior, I have never taken any risks and have never allowed anyone to get close to me until now...

"Two cents for your thoughts Empress?" Marcus says opening the balcony door and smiling at me.

"Actually, Marcus come and join me outside, I need to ask you something, Honey."

20 ~ CHARMAINE

As exhausted as I am from the events of the day, It is after 2 am when I retire to bed. Earlier I accompanied our driver Lennox to take Junior to Montego Bay. On the way back, I decide to sit up front to benefit from the window being open and from the running jokes he's giving me about who lives in the big houses as he points out places of interest along the way.

Medina has already sprayed my room with insect repellent for the night, I have a shower and apply repellent to my skin, and I put on the long sleeved pyjamas I ordered from Mum's catalogue. My nighttime dilemma returns, should I open the window facing the garden and risk the mosquitoes skydiving into my bedroom and feasting on my body during the night? Or should I switch the fan on high and listen to it whirling, pushing hot air around the room. The way my luck is going I am probably going to stay hot all night and get eaten too. I let out a sigh and sit on the bed taking a pause from dragging everything out of my case to find something I haven't worn yet to the Homecoming BBQ tomorrow and decide to call my Mum.

I grab my mobile phone from the bedside table, where I left it plugged in and charging all day. I can see it's after 2 am here in Jamaica so by my reckoning it's about 7 am in the UK. I dial her number and I make myself comfortable on my side of the bed. My side of the bed...I have been sleeping on the right-hand side of the bed for six years and even though Junior is staying overnight with friends in Montego Bay, I cannot sleep in the middle of the bed where I would be much more comfortable. I feel like I have always been on the edges of Junior's life, I don't know his family or his friends for that matter. Junior is always falling out with everybody including me. Since we've been here I have been out once with Junior to visit relatives on his father's side. They appeared to be good people, in the church and everything but it is not how I imagined my first visit to Jamaica would be.

Even though I have never stayed in a hotel I can imagine those people who we saw on the plane are out sipping cocktails, sunbathing, and enjoying the nightlife. I will have to link up with Marcus and make sure I see more of the island while I am here. Lord knows when I will be able to afford to come back to Jamaica. I can hear the international ringing tone and I wait for Mum's face to pop up on my screen.

"Hey, Mum! How are you doing? How are the twins?"

Mum is clearly visible on my mobile phone screen, she's on the floor in her bathroom and I can hear the twins splashing about in the bath.

"I'm not too bad Charms and the children are fine. In fact, they are a pleasure to look after. I can really see the difference since you completed the parenting course. They have been going to sleep at 7 o'clock most evenings, I'm just getting them ready washed and dressed now then I'll get them so breakfast"

"That is wonderful to hear Mum," I reply, "You know I didn't like being referred like that and I wasn't looking forward to attending, but it was a really good course."

Apart from bathing the twins, I could tell quite instinctively that Mum was pre-occupied like something was bothering her, but I did not want to push it by asking.

"How was the funeral?" Mum enquired.

"It was a lovely send off. Very fitting for the kind of man he was and very well attended, the church was packed with people."

"Ok, Good!" Mum said pensively.

I decided to leave out the moment when Junior tried to jump on top of the coffin at the graveside and Rose 'fainting' as it was too long to explain via Skype. But first thing when I get back, we will sit with a cup of tea and the coconut Gizzada Medina makes, (which happens to be Mums favourite cake) and we'll have a good old chinwag and a much-needed catch-up. I am really looking forward to going home.

"So, what's the weather like?" Mum interrupted my thoughts.

"Oh, the weather's gloriously hot during the day, but sticky and close at night. Hardly any rain at all, so it looks like we'll have the perfect day for the Homegoing BBQ tomorrow. I have been running on the beach most mornings before the sun gets too hot and Marcus has joined me a couple of times as well."

"Well done Charms', I know you're there to support Junior and his family, but I am glad you are getting a little break as well. How are you and Junior doing at the moment?"

"The same as we were in London Mum, no change. He's been out most nights in Negril raving with his friends." I reply despondently.

"I am so disappointed for you Charms; I was hoping that you two being away in another environment like beautiful Jamaica, might have sparked a reconciliation," Mum said hopefully. That's when I knew something was up. Mum had been worse towards Junior since he was arrested and now she was behaving like he and she are friends?

"Really Mum? You want me and Junior to get back together?" "It would have been nice," Mum said sadly, "I love you Charms," Mum added.

Now I was spooked as the last time she said those words to me was after I had given birth to the twins. Don't get me wrong, my Mum loves me, but I was Daddy's princess and it's taken a lot of hard work to mend our relationship after my antics when he died. Mum and I are close, but we don't do random 'I Love Yous' unless someone's sick.

"Mum are you sure you're ok?" I say in a panic, "Are the twins ill?" I add frantically.

"I am fine and so are the twins. If we were ill I would have told you."

I was unconvinced, "Then what is it Mum, you look like you're going to cry?" I say sitting upright and swinging my legs off the bed.

"Ok, just promise me you won't get angry or upset?"

"Mum, what the hell is going on there? Do I need to come home because I'm stranded here for the next two weeks?" There was silence before Mum let out a deep sigh whilst I held my breath.

"Do you remember that white woman that Junior had the affair with?"

I exhaled, "Of course I do! I'm not about to forget her, am I! Why?"

"Charmaine, the woman went to your house yesterday looking for Junior. Marcia gave her my address and she came straight over to me,"

I sensed my blood pressure and my temper rising, "What the hell did Marcia do that for?" followed by a few curse words under my breath.

"Well, I had no choice but to let her in,"

"What for Mum? Junior told me that after the court case that he and she was done! History!"

"Charmaine Maxine Morgan! Will you let me finish?" It was more of a command than a request which silenced me immediately.

"I'm sorry Mum do continue."

"No, I'm sorry Charmaine…I am sorry to have to tell you that Mandy is pregnant, she's eight months gone, and she said Junior is her baby father."

There she said it. It took me a hot minute for what Mum said to register, then it hit me like a power surge through the phone; I felt I had to drop it to avoid being electrocuted. The phone slipped out of my hand in slow motion hitting the side of the bedframe smashing the screen before hitting the marble floor. I saw Mum's image for a further few seconds before her face faded into the darkness, I threw myself back on the bed sobbing, clutching my chest as it felt like my heart was going to physically break out of my body into a thousand pieces. I could easily get the screen repaired but my heart was still fragile from Junior's affair. I cried myself to sleep then woke up suddenly because I had been bitten by a mosquito on my arm even through my pyjama sleeve. The darker the night became the darker my anger and my mood. I thought about the promises we made to each other on our wedding day.... until death do us part, so there will be no divorce for us. Then as the sun arose it dawned on me, Charmaine there's more than one way to end a marriage...

...I then raised my left hand and forcefully smashed myself on the right arm. I lifted my left hand from my right forearm to reveal, a very large, dead mosquito.

Later that morning, I ran along the beach as fast as I could for a solid 40 minutes passing all of the posh hotels on the right with the beach and the Caribbean Sea on the left. At this time of the morning, there were no guests by the pool or on the beach. The closed parasols, loungers and chairs stood erected standing to attention. The hotel workers busy cleaning the resort and folding towels getting ready for the day. Nobody minded that I was running through the property, as joggers were commonplace at that time. The sweat was pouring down my face and sweat patches were coming through on my T-shirt on my armpits; all signs I was burning calories. I glanced at the App on my broken screen on my phone to confirm that not only had I lost a lot of kcals, I had already run 10,000 steps and it wasn't even 7 o'clock in the morning yet. I took a couple of sips of water and decided to head back. Today was going to be a busy day in the Morgan household and we were going to meet Marcus' girlfriend. Apparently, she had already been here a week but didn't think it was appropriate to meet Marcus' family for the first time at the funeral and I already respected her for that. I was running on the sand like an expert now, saying good morning to the vendors setting up their stalls, handmade jewellery, wooden carvings and cheap souvenirs. When I got to my junction, I noticed the old Rasta was not there. To be honest, I was relieved, he always had something crass to say to jar me and I was reaching the point when I wanted to tell him two bad words. I jogged across the road and I could see a large truck at the house and a lot of activity. I assumed the chairs for the Homegoing had arrived.

I said, "Good morning." to the neighbours who were picking fruit and vegetables from their allotment on the roundabout and jogged around the house passing the verandah, to the back of the house. I recognised a couple of the men who had carried out our luggage out of the taxi when we first arrived. They looked like they had everything in hand. Neighbours had already set up the gazebo, which would house the buffet tables and chafing dishes. I also saw a huge oil drum barbeque and a spit roast being set up further down the yard. At the verandah at the back of the bungalow, I saw and heard Junior setting up the PA system. He was being assisted by the old Rastaman who had an old drum with him. I climbed the stairs quickly to avoid them both.

Once inside I could smell the aroma of the start of a good curried goat and my stomach rumbled automatically to remind me that other than a handful of sea grapes I had not eaten breakfast. I took off my sweaty trainers and carried them through to my room, then I entered the bathroom briefly to wash my hands and face. I then joined Medina and Mother Morgan at the kitchen table.

"Good morning, ladies," I said happily greeting Mother Morgan with a kiss on the cheek.

"Good morning my darling, enjoy your exercise?" She replied.

"Would you like a cup of tea Miss Charmaine?" asked Medina, "De kettle just boil!"

"Only if you're making one yourself. I've said it before Medina, please call me Charmaine."

"Very well Miss Charmaine." she smiled, and we all chuckled.

"We have a lot of work to do before the congregation from Kingston arrive, fancy giving us a hand Charmaine. Many hands make light work?"

Mother Morgan's tone was soft and warm. I looked at Medina to get her approval and she nodded in agreement too. After tea and toast, Medina set up the table with chopping boards, bowls of water and some of the sharpest knives I have ever seen. I had to peel and dice the potatoes to make potato salad, then peel and chop carrots, grate white cabbages and scallions to make the coleslaw. Mother Morgan and I made small talk about her late husband mainly and about my children. I had seen them on Skype earlier and they were behaving for my Mum. I was missing them now. As Medina went to wash my potatoes at the sink, I was making a start on the carrots. We were in the zone and I was just enjoying the company of the older women.

"I blame myself you know!" Mother Morgan admitted.

I looked at her puzzled but figured she would explain.

"I blame myself for how Junior turned out...

...when Carlos was posted to London to head up the church in Battersea I should have insisted that the three boys came with us. But we were not sure what we were coming to, up in England. We ended up lodging in a room in somebody else's home; not really suitable for a very young family. I left the boys with my parents where they would get the best upbringing in the countryside. Junior was a baby, my washbelly. He was a beautiful baby Charmaine, so much like the baby photos you sent me of Garrison," She said reminiscing, "As we got more established and bought our first home I got the paperwork and money together to send for Manley. He was already a teenager by the time he came up and he went straight into secondary school. Poor lamb, he found it so difficult to fit in at school in England. So, we worked quite quickly to get Marcus over so he could benefit from a primary school education before going to grammar school. Then my father died suddenly, and I came home for his funeral. When I arrived, Junior didn't recognise me, and he wouldn't leave his grandmother's lap no matter how hard she tried to coax him. He wasn't having it."

Mother Morgan tossed the diced beetroot into the bowl of water and picked up another, "He must have been five or six years old at the time; the rejection broke my heart. After the funeral when I said I wanted to take him to the UK, my Mother and I had a row and she persuaded me to let her raise him in Jamaica. That was the biggest mistake of my life and my biggest regret. With his 'gran gran' all to himself, he was spoilt rotten and he ran rings around her, by that time she was a frail old woman. Soon the school was writing to me about this bad behaviour, whilst he excelled at playing the guitar and singing, his behaviour in the classroom got worse and worse. As a teenager, he refused to go to church preferring to travel into Kingston with some older boys going into some dangerous areas to go to dances or recording studios. Carlos was so focused on building the church and winning over the lost at any cost, he couldn't see that we were losing our own child.

Eventually, Junior stopped coming to the phone to speak to me; not to even to say thanks for the money I religiously sent to him. Junior jumped at the chance to come to London on a six-month visa to cut a reggae album though and the plan was for him to go back to Jamaica. We met him at the airport, and I was shocked to see that he had started to grow dreadlocks and he stunk heavily of cannabis. I was so embarrassed, but as my Mother would say, "yuh mek the pickney but you don't make its mind." She paused. "Did you know he brought that stuff into our home?" She asked. I shook my head in indignation and reached for the grater to start shredding the cabbages. "Yes Charmaine, Carlos was invited to preach at one of our churches in Wales, so we took Manley as he had given his heart to the Lord and was considering baptism. We decided to stay overnight in Cardiff town centre, at a lovely bed and breakfast near the church. Marcus had gone on a trip to Germany with the school so Junior was left home alone. When we got back reggae music was blaring out of my front room. Our neighbours informed me that surprisingly there had been a party on Friday night. Junior was the only person in the property, and he was sitting in my front room smoking drugs! Charmaine, you should have seen the state of my front room! The sight of it made me feel sick to the pit of my stomach. This was my best room, this was the room where I received people from the church, where we had prayer meeting and now it was covered in a layer of ash over the carpet, the sofa and all of my little nic nacs that I'd collected and treasured over the years. Our home stunk to high heaven of ganja smoke, the smell was even ingrained into the soft furnishings. I knew I would have to throw everything out including my beautiful nets and heavy curtains."

Mother Morgan looking so upset sighed as she drew breath and then she continued, "Junior, my son, had turned my home into a drugs den and he really couldn't care less. His eyes were red, bloodshot and his body language told me that he found the whole scene he had created quite amusing. There was no sorry, no remorse, no shame. The disrespect was blatant, and my husband wasn't pleased at all. Carlos lifted his fists and launched at Junior knocking him out of the armchair to the ground, unshaken Junior arose quickly and fought back punching his dad on the jaw. A father and his son fighting like Mohammed Ali and Joe Frazier. I tried to jump in to stop them, but Junior pushed me over, this only made things worse. I was screaming and begging at them to stop; for someone to intervene to help me separate them. My back was to my husband and I was facing Junior pleading with him to calm down and then he said, 'I suspected you would side with him like you sided with him all the time.' I asked him what he was talking about and he said, 'You know you've always sided with him over me why should I expect anything different now?' Junior looked at me with disgust and I could feel the hatred in his heart almost like he couldn't understand why we would be angry that he had desecrated our home...

...My husband shouted words to the effect of 'one of us needs to leave this house right now and it's not going to be me.' And that's when Junior said, 'that's ok I'll go, I'll leave, you never wanted me here in the first place right from the beginning, you left me in Jamaica with gran gran and you didn't look back!' I tried to explain how hard it was to leave him there, but he wouldn't listen to reason. 'I'm out of this place once and for all and I'm never coming back' he shouted, his words broke my heart and I dropped to my knees holding onto his leg begging him to stay. 'Mum,' he said, 'when I needed you, you just wasn't there. You don't know what I had to endure in Jamaica!' Now I was confused. I asked him what happened, suddenly sober and coherent, he said, 'it doesn't matter anymore,' but it did matter, he's my child, my baby."

I tell you, when Mother Morgan shared what Junior had been through, I couldn't believe my ears. Junior told her words to the effect of, "Mum, your baby was molested, messed about with and assaulted sexually, every day from the time you left me until I stopped going to flipping Sunday school!"

Mother Morgan said he just kept swearing, he was so angry and eventually, he stormed out of the room.

"Charmaine the news stopped me and his father in our tracks. This was the last thing I was expecting Junior to tell us, but I knew that he was telling the truth. My mind went back to the scandal that came to light a few years ago when the children now adults jointly told the authorities about historic child sexual abuse. The man was a Sunday school teacher. Of course, he denied it and there was a huge investigation with other victims coming forward. Junior was already in the UK during the case, so I wrongly assumed nothing happened to him, how wrong

I was. With the mounting allegations and subsequent court case, the perpetrator was found guilty and sentenced to 14 years in prison. It also was revealed that he had been raping his sons and daughters.

That minister raped my Junior, fourteen years was not long enough for what he did, but I will forever be guilty of leaving my child behind, leaving him to endure horror upon horror at his tender age." Mother Morgan with tears streaming down her face spoke in whispers so that she wasn't overheard by Medina or anybody else in the vicinity. I cried inside for Junior as I was fighting hard to suppress my own tears from falling. "Yes, damaged goods, Charmaine and angry with the whole world." she then cautioned me saying, "Don't let him take it out on you Charmaine, you didn't hurt him! You deserve to be happy!"

21~ ROSE

I t is a glorious sunny day and the yard has been decorated beautifully for the Homegoing barbecue everything from napkins to balloons was either royal blue white or gold. I wish my camera took nice photos because my Mum would really like to see this. For most celebrations, at home or at church my Mum would ask what the colour scheme was or propose a colour scheme for an event. She liked things looking uniform.

So, at the last blessing where she catered for a baby girl it was pale pink, white and silver balloons with pink and gold napkins and she made and decorated a two-tiered pink and white christening rum cake. The christening party all wore white including the godparents and the couple's other two children. The church hall was transformed and had the wow factor. My Mum just had a flair for all things decadent yet tasteful so this event in the Morgan's backyard was something I knew she would appreciate.

I estimate there are about 60 people in all who have come across from Kingston to Negril to celebrate the life of Overseer Morgan. The barbecue is blazing, and Manley is in charge of grilling the meat and fish. Junior is entertaining the gathering on the verandah where he has created a little stage with speakers and a backing track system. He's singing all of Pops Morgan's favourite choruses from yesteryear in a reggae style and the old Rasta is beating his African drum in tune going off in his own zone with his dreadlocks shaking all over the place. The way they are carrying on you'd think they were the opening act at Reggae Sun Splash or Glastonbury.

"What a racket!" Mother Morgan made her entrance via the back door and she immediately indicated to Junior that he needed to turn the backing music down so she could hear herself think and Junior turned down the volume immediately. Mother Morgan collected herself and she climbed down the verandah steps holding on to the rail, making small talk with her guests and moving gracefully around the backyard giving hugs to whoever needed them. She looked a little frail but beautiful in black slacks and a very fussy black blouse. She wore her trademark mother of pearl brooch and no other jewellery apart from her engagement, wedding and eternity rings. Years before just before they left the UK to retire in Jamaica, Mother Morgan had promised to leave her engagement ring to me when she died and her wedding ring to Charmaine. Her emerald encrusted eternity ring was for Marcus' wife whenever that happened.

As if on cue, Marcus makes a grand entry with three other people, two women and a young man with an acoustic guitar. Marcus is at least three shades darker, having caught the sun. He goes directly to his mother and introduces his group to her. I think to myself this must be Marcus' new girlfriend, her mother and perhaps her brother and I move quickly towards them navigating all the chairs and people so I could have an audience with them. I think to myself rather judgmentally I know that Marcus is a decent man but what kind of mother would allow her young daughter to date a man many times her senior, she looks no more than 20 years old, a baby.

After their brief conversation, Mother Morgan is beaming from ear to ear like she has just been told excellent news. Marcus looks ever so happy too. Infectiously, I start smiling at them. Charmaine joins us eating a plate of ackee and saltfish. I swear that girl loves her food too much! Marcus grabs the older woman's hand and he introduces her as his fiancée. I'm quite shocked and I cannot conceal just how shocked I am.

Marcus' fiancée is wearing a beautiful off-white linen shift trouser suit and her sisterlocs are wrapped in a beautiful African print headwrap with matching bangles and loop earrings in the same print. Her name is Patti, she looks so regal. I gather quite quickly that the younger woman is, in fact, her daughter Yolanda, who is stunningly beautiful, like her mother. Well, the lime does not fall far from the tree! She has certainly inherited her mother's good genes. The young man is Yolanda's 'friend' Jaylen a musician from the hotel where they have been staying. I am confused about how Marcus' partner was a girlfriend last week and his fiancée this week, but I'm sure Marcus will explain it all. Mother Morgan appears to be delighted at the news and gives her approval by embracing Patti tightly. Charmaine stops eating and puts out her hand to shake their hands and I do the same. She points Jaylen towards the stage and he goes over to jam with Junior and the old Rasta. I laugh when I see Junior beating the tambourine, only God knows where he got that from, it must have been from someone in the congregation from Kingston church. The people are clearly enjoying the trip down memory lane as they are standing, singing along, clapping and dancing, it's a beautiful sight to see. Overseer Morgan was very much loved by his congregation. Marcus approaches the stage and asks for the microphone from Junior, they hug as Junior hands it over.

"My dear family and friends. Thank you for travelling across from Kingston church to share this day with us. Thank you for your support today and I thank you for your support in the coming weeks. My Mum will certainly need it." He paused. "To everybody else, he was called Overseer or Pastor; to his work colleagues, he was Mr Morgan. His close friends got to call him Carlos and Mummy called him a lot of names when she was cross!" Everybody looked at Mother Morgan and laughed she was laughing too. "No, seriously folks, my Mum called my Dad her sweetheart, they honoured their wedding vows until death and that's what I want folks, a marriage until death parts us. I am not trying to steal the limelight here, but I have already spoken to Mum and she has given her blessing to share my news with you...Come up here Patti." Patti joined Marcus on the veranda. He took a deep breath and said, "Everybody please say hi to my beautiful

Empress Patti Scotland...we are getting married here in Negril next week."

Poor Patti looked like she would faint in the heat as he placed his mother's engagement ring on her finger and passionately kissed her. Everybody cheered and applauded but Manley didn't look too pleased at all. He promptly turned back to his brother, furiously turning over the BBQ chicken on the grill then slamming down the lid. He probably wished that as the eldest brother, Marcus had introduced his fiancée to him first or maybe it was because some strange brown-skinned woman was wearing his mother's ring. Whatever it was Manley was cross about, he would soon let Marcus know when the family was alone. So, the Homegoing Celebration was turning into an impromptu engagement party. Marcus made a point of introducing Patti to everybody present, they warm to her instantly, all except Manley who is focused on the task of cooking the food and making sure everybody eats.

Junior ended the evening with his reggae hit from the 90's which was all about love and was well received by the congregation. Everybody filed out and left with something whether it be containers of food, cake or both. There was plenty of it and no way we could eat it all even though we were staying for another week. I congratulate Marcus and Patti with a kiss on both cheeks, telling them I am so happy for them and excited for their future. I ask Patti what she does for a living and she duly explains that she works for the Probation Service in North London. Marcus volunteers that she also works with perpetrators and victims of domestic violence, that disclosure troubles my spirit. I recognise it was not a coincidence meeting Patti today; she was destined to be here in Jamaica at this point in time. We were destined to meet, and I know that Patti was the one sent to save me, I wonder if she knew that the Lord had sent her to me?

22~ PATTI

"Cheese on bread man! Cheese on bread! But what de ass you telling me this good Sunday afternoon? I'm here now coming in from church trying to steam a little bit of rice to go with the fried chicken from yesterday. I really don't understand you Patti Scotland, you're studying to gain your PhD you're a bright, intelligent, smart woman yet you behave like you went to school at the standpipe! Get married to who doh Patti? You only met the man de other day pon de train and now you're getting married next week? What the ass is the rush for do, na? You pregnant?" Veronica asks. But she does not wait for me to answer. "No, you can't be pregnant? You're too old for that now," she concludes.

"Charming Mum!" I reply but she is not listening to me at all. From experience, once Veronica loses her temper, her Barbadian accent becomes more prominent and she uses a lot of old-fashioned Bajan proverbs and does not listen to anything you may have to say.

"Well he can't be marrying you for your burgundy passport because he done have his papers already and he travels all over de place. If his papers weren't in good order he wouldn't have been able to leave the country to attend his father's funeral." She reasoned with herself, "So, please Patti what's the big hurry? What did Yolanda say when you told her your news? Wait, hold on don't bother to answer, she's probably just happy she's going to be your bridesmaid. She's away with the fairies that one. So, what did Ms Antoinette have to say she's got a lot of sense that one, I bet she didn't approve of this foolishness?" Mum demands an answer.

"Well, she has her reservations Mum, but at the end of the day, it's my decision to make and she supports me wholeheartedly." I try to say bravely.

There's silence as both of us gather our thoughts. I can see Veronica turning off the stove under the rice, then she positions the tablet on the dining room table so we can see each other. She claps her hands together once then she exclaims, "I know what he wants from you Patti, it just occurred to me he wants your bloody house! Remember Ms Maud? The St Lucian lady who used to work down at Queen's hospital?" She asked.

"Not really Mum," I say,

"You can't remember she was a midwife for a number of years before retiring when she was 60? Used to bake the best coconut bread in East London?"

"Oh yes, I remember her now Mum, why what happened to her?"

"Well, I was just going to tell you! Anyway, she retired as I said at 60 years old and went down to St Lucia Jazz Festival a couple of years ago playing young and wukking up she self on the People's catamaran trip and wining up she self at every pot that lick. She met this local St Lucian bwoy with a slim body and coolie hair and she came back to London telling everybody who would listen that she had fallen in love with a man about 30 years her junior. The following year she went down to St Lucia and got married to him on the beach and she wore white! I swear all that man brought to the relationship was his suitcase, his PlayStation and good sex. He refused to work saying there was nothing that matched his skill set as a beach bum and he stayed in the marriage for exactly two years, then he told her he wanted a family and she was too old to do that. Done. Rumour has it he already had his woman up here in Hayes. But because he was in the marriage for two years he knew that he was entitled to half of her house and she had to buy him out. Now she's doing agency work at a time when she should be relaxing and enjoying her retirement. Ms Maud was the talk of the African Caribbean Club for months after that. I'm sorry to have to tell you this Patti but Marcus Morgan is after your house; your little legacy for my granddaughter." Veronica sat back in the dining room chair like she just uncovered the crime of the century, with a satisfied look on her face.

"Mum, I doubt Marcus is interested in my little two up two down he has a property portfolio of about 20 homes across London we're going to come to an agreement that my house stays my home and will go to Yolanda in due course."

"Oh, I didn't realise that," Mum said.

"Well, Mum every time he came to your home in the last three months you've made up an excuse to leave the room and not get to know him." I reasoned.

"Now that's not fair!" Mum interrupted, "You know how bad my headaches can get. At no point in the last three months did I realise that you and Marcus were that serious about each other. What does his family think? Have you even met his family?" She inquired.

"I met them at the Homegoing barbecue yesterday

they're good people." I summarised.

"And how on earth do you know that after meeting them once? They could be a bunch of criminals?"

"They are church people Mum, Marcus comes from a line of ministers, his brother is a pastor, his dad was overseer of the church and his dad and his dad before him."

"Oh shite! they're the worst!" said Mum. "Minister's children always turn out the worse. Is there any way that someone can check out the family just in case?" she asked.

"Whatever do you mean Mum?"

"Well, before your time and before my time every village had an old wise woman. The woman in my district of College Savannah St John was called Mudda. Mudda must have been at least 100 years old, nobody recalled her ever being young she was always old. Nobody knew her real name. To everybody in the village, she was simply Mudda and she earned that title because she delivered practically every baby in the village. She had many roles because back then you couldn't afford to go to the doctor unless you had money, so she was a midwife.

She dabbled with the herbs a bit, so if you had a

cold or a cut that wouldn't heal she would tell you which leaves to go and pick and where to pick them from and then she would mix up her little lotions and potions and when you followed her instructions you always got better.

One of her other jobs was washing dead bodies and preparing them for burial. Somebody once told me that she was cleaning a dead body of a woman and she couldn't get to a particular area of the body and she asked the corpse to help her and the body moved! Well, that would have scared me shitless," Mum cackled with laughter, showing me all of her false teeth.

"One very important aspect of her role was when she was appointed by a potential bride's family to check out the groom's family. You see back in the day men would travel from plantation to plantation to work the fields cutting sugar cane, from time to time they would spend time working at other plantations working away from home for long periods of time. It wasn't uncommon for the men to start new families elsewhere in the island; the role of a Mudda would be to check out whether or not the bride and groom were, in fact, brother and sister. Now before you start, I know that you and Marcus are not related, your family hail from West

Africa but Mudda would also check out if there was any genetic flaws in the family. She would travel incognito pretending to be interested in buying land nearby the groom's family and she would ask questions regarding the family's lineage, mental health or criminal activities. Mudda and other women like her were the original Olivia Pope without the nice clothes bags and shoes. They were keepers of our culture, historians, fixers, financial advisors, healthcare assistants and investigators. I wish you had a Mudda around now because no family including Marcus' are that perfect Patti, none."

When I looked at Mum, she looked exhausted she had her hands to her temple rubbing her head, a sure sign that the onslaught of another headache was coming.

"Mum, Marcus is here, he's been listening the whole time. Do you want to speak to him?"

"Okay then. Hi Marcus."

"Hi Mum Veronica, well we're not married yet so what else would you want to know Miss Veronica?"

"I don't want to know anything more, to be honest, I just wanted to apologise if I've said anything out of turn especially about your dearly departed father and your mother. It's just that I have fostered many children over the last 40 odd years but as you know I've had Patti from birth, and I adopted her when she turned 18 years old. Children came and children left their placements with me, but it's really only been Patti and I and I love her dearly."

"I can tell you, Miss Veronica, that I love your daughter very, very much and I love Yolanda like a daughter, I would never ever do anything to harm them, I just feel blessed that Patti has come into my life right now. I was very surprised when she proposed to me, but it was just a matter of time, in fact, she beat me to it, I would have proposed to her eventually." He said smugly.

"Shut the front door! What the ass is it you're telling me? Patti proposed to you. Put her raas back on this Skype call immediately Marcus Morgan!

Patti Scotland! I'm booking on the next flight to Kingston, I need to find out what the raas is going on out der!" screamed Veronica

My friend Bev from the office is on the dance floor and since she arrived at the hotel the male staff have been calling her Fluffy Diva and she's loving the attention. She's been dancing away to Jamaican dancehall classics with the hotel manager Derrick and she hasn't looked back for me once. I didn't even know that she liked Reggae music. The truth is I'm jealous, it's my hen do, and tonight is about me not her!

Yolanda is chatting away by the pool with Jaylen, the drummer from the band Tranzishan. I'm even jealous of her too because she's young and having a holiday romance...I feel so old. The band have just finished their set and are taking a well-deserved break.

Charmaine is nursing a Bob Marley cocktail and as soon as I tell her the drinks are free she is actively working her way through the cocktail menu and getting merrier in her seat. I'm jealous of her too as I can't cut loose and get drunk.

Rose looks as uncomfortable as a nun in a brothel, everything about her body language is screaming that she doesn't want to be here in this den of iniquity and I feel like Billy no mates.

I can hear my Mum bossing someone around before I can see her and when she comes into view she is wearing a bright orange kaftan dress with a matching turban; she looks so regal like a Bajan queen. Mum is being escorted to where we are sitting by a member of staff.

"Bless you, hun," she says endearingly, "Patti, give this helpful young gentleman a tip for me please, I didn't get the chance to change up any money yet." I give him a US dollar from my purse, and he hurries away trying to get away before Mum could ask for help with anything else.

"Good evening Mum, thanks for coming," I say.

It is dark outside with just tea lights on the table and white fairy lights clinging to the palm trees above. The moonlight and stars light up the open spaces at the back of the hotel. Even so, I can clearly see my Mother's neck and chest is cased with talcum powder but for what purpose I do not know. I thought to myself, "she's always so extra."

"Rose and Charmaine, I'd like to introduce you to my Mother," I say.

"Good evening" they both reply in unison.

"Good night, my name is Veronica Scotland," she says rising briefly to shake their hands. Turning to me she says under her breath, "Patti I don't feel…feel…" and as if by magic she produces her Vicks nasal spray and expertly places the tube into her nostril and inhales like her life depends on it. "I must have caught a chill on the plane earlier today," Veronica confesses.

"Awww Mum I'm sorry to hear that," I respond with all the sympathy I can muster.

"Yes child, I got a bad feeling all over my body...I soon dead." As soon as she said that all sympathy for Veronica vanished. My Mum had been dying for the last 15 years, but yet for her age she was strong as an Ox. Every six months she would have her check up at the well women's clinic to be told other than laying off consuming too much salt, she was in good shape. It used to really upset me and Yolanda when she started this 'soon dead' stuff but it didn't bother me anymore, 'Veronica Hyacinth Scotland will outlive everybody sitting here,' I think to myself.

"Shall I get someone to call a doctor for you Mum?" I ask, feigning concern.

"No Hun, I don't want to be any bother. I've asked the young man to get me some Bay Rum. I'll dip some in a cloth and tie my head and try to sleep it off." She says rising.

"Ok, Mum if you need anything just call me on my mobile phone. Night, night Mum," I reply. She waves to Rose and Charmaine until she catches their attention and then she walks through the hotel foyer to the lifts as majestically as she had entered.

A little time and a few virgin pina colada's later, Ann graces us with her presence. She is dressed in a white

T-shirt and white linen shorts, clearly not dressed for the evening's entertainment at the hotel, My heart sinks. She says, "Hi," to the ladies and sits where Veronica had been sitting, "Babes, I can't stop long at all, Elijah won't settle, he slept most of the way here from the airport. Malakai has gone out with Marcus and I only booked the babysitting service for a few minutes," she pauses, "so sorry but I really have to go!"

"Ann, you can't stop and have a one drink with me?" I said pouting like Yolanda, curling my bottom lip.

"No," she says sharply, "I don't want to leave Elijah, we're not the McCann's! Besides that, I really have to leave now!"

She gets out of her seat and promptly leaves to go back inside the hotel complex. And then the penny drops, I finally get the memo. Years ago, we developed the saying, "I really have to leave now!" It meant that our professional world and our personal world had collided. I first coined the phrase when I was a newly qualified Probation officer. I had written a Pre-Sentence Report on a man from Grenada, I'll never forget him, there are some punters that stay with you. He appeared in Court for an offence of drink driving, about 104 on the breathalyser, almost three times the legal limit. He was a chef by profession and had his own catering company. I proposed a combination order comprising of supervision and 100 hours of community service and the magistrates duly followed my proposal. It was during supervision sessions with me that he finally admitted that he and his team would set up the function or event, serve the food and after the event, drink off all of the leftover beers, wines and spirits, meaning he had driven drunk nearly every night since he started his company two years ago.

Cutting a long story short, a few weeks later I was invited to my good friend's birthday party at Zars Zars in Stratford and I was getting ready to order some food and guess who comes out of the kitchen all sweaty and stressed? My client. He was mortified when he saw me and I was so shocked when I saw him that the menu no longer looked appetising and I told Ann that we needed to leave, "We really have to leave now!" Another time we were at Notting Hill Carnival Ann and I were in our camouflage shorts and ripped up matching tops and had black war paint on our faces displaying no behaviour and we were just about to pass the judges platform with our chocolate, paint and powder when Ann shouts at me over the music. "I've got to go; I really have to leave now!" I was vex but knew we couldn't get caught on social media wukking up with the local gangsters she was representing. And now Ann had bumped into one of her clients at this hotel in Jamaica! What were the odds on that? It could only be Rose or Charmaine that she recognised, and my money was on Charmaine. I'll get Ann to give me the lowdown later. For now, the DJ calling my name and playing the introduction to the Candy Song interrupts my thoughts. Yolanda is screaming,

"Come on Mum!" as she jumps up instantly ready to do the formation and Jaylen follows her to the dance floor. Beverley has unlocked herself from Derrick who is now off duty and organises everybody into rows. Rose point blank refuses to get involved but Charmaine leads me to the dance floor like we were old mates. Yolanda insists that I be at the front as the DJ starts the song again and we dance. Later, he plays all of my favourite tunes from back in the day, Lover's rock classics like Carol Thompson and Janet Kay. We dance the whole night, with other hotel guests joining in. We sing, 'Silly Games' at the top of our voices, cracking up laughing at the high notes that none of us can reach. When it's time for the band to come on we sit down at our table exhausted.

Rose is as serious as a judge, but we ignore her and order another round of drinks. The band start their repertoire of Bob Marley classics and we are singing along at our table. No Woman, No Cry and Redemption Song are instant hits with the guests. Beverley resumes slow dancing with Derrick and Yolanda sits on the edge of the stage swooning over Jaylen. All I can see are his teeth smiling as he plays the drums in the dark.

As the vocalist and lead guitarist introduce the next song, Rose stands up with her hands flat on the table and yells, "I am so sorry to say this as you are about to marry Marcus, but we've been wanting to talk to you all night"

"Not right now Rose, it can wait!" interjects Charmaine.

"No, it can't!" says Rose and before Charmaine can calm Rose down she screams, "We want to leave our husbands and we need you to help us!"

Everyone freezes in silence, the band, the hotel staff, even Beverley stops dancing. Like I said at the beginning, some hen party this is turning out to be!

23 ~ CHARMAINE

"Wow, Rose rolls up and she drops the mike on Patti like a boss! I laugh until I cry..."

24 ~ ROSE

"If you're going to pray and worry, don't pray". Rose Morgan.

Loving the Brothers

Pamela R Haynes

www.lovingthebrothers.org

VOLUME TWO

~

Loving the Sisters ...

1~PATTI

After three long weeks in Jamaica I was dreading going back to work. I knew I would be fine once I got there but I really got used to being a lady of leisure. I did not sleep very well at all. I had been fretting about the disclosures that Rose and Charmaine had made at the hen party...who knew! I was not keen on getting involved but I could not get out it. Rose was saying that I was chosen but I didn't feel I had a choice. I hate having a caseload in my personal life. That's why very few people even know what I do for a living. My job is stressful enough without having casework after hours too. I was also fretting about work. I guessed my email box was jammed to capacity and my in-tray was full of work to complete as we were preparing for another inspection. My first meeting of the day was going to be at HQ with my line manager then I would make my way to the office and catch up with my team. I had a few snaps of our wedding on my mobile phone and

Jamaican souvenirs for everybody. Beverley came back on the same flight as us and she had a few days extra at home to recover from travelling.

Marcus was already up and out to the gym before going to Wembley stadium to join a team of other engineers to prepare for the Rod Stewart concert later that evening. He had kissed me on my lips in my sleep with his dreadlocks caressing my forehead, which made me wake up momentarily. When I glanced drowsily over at the alarm clock it was just after 5 am. I growled and pulled the duvet over my head and drifted back off to sleep. It felt like I had closed my eyes for a couple of seconds and the alarm went off signalling that it was 7 am and Mrs Patti Scotland-Morgan had to get her butt in gear and get ready for work. I tugged on my dressing gown and went downstairs to the kitchen. On route, I saw Marcus' shoes in the hall and his coat on the stand and it warmed my heart.

We decided he would move in with Yolanda and I. He was going to rent out his flat at some stage and probably sell one of his properties later down the line and then we'd buy a place together. Given Veronica's fears about Marcus' evil intentions of ripping me off, he wanted his solicitors to draft papers ensuring my house went to

Yolanda. He reasoned the way things were going economically this was the only way she would become a homeowner.

Now, that's what I love about Marcus he was always thinking of us, open and transparent. I stared at his mother's ring on my left hand as I clasped my cup of red berry tea and I growled out loud. I was only a couple of weeks into my marriage and I was already keeping a big secret from my husband…

COMING SOON

Publishers Afterword

For over six months, my favourite line has been **"I'm Loving, Loving the Brothers"**. My team members would look at me and smile, huge wide grins, as they knew what I was talking about. It has been an immense pleasure and honour working with Pamela R Haynes on her first fiction novel. Working with Pam was an epic creative challenge during which, Pam was completely open to our suggestions and feedback. She interpreted our guidance and our exploration of the story and then went swiftly to work on writing additional chapters and extensions to build the book.

Pam has worked diligently to make her mark in this craft we call writing. Pam has a gift and it shines through the words she has set on paper. Loving The Brothers is written purposefully with domestic violence and sexual violence as main features. This book helps us to see how abuse, societal pressures and a lack of knowledge can impair the quality of our relationships. In Patti, we see a woman who can and will make a difference in supporting and empowering other women. I am keen to see how the characters both male and female are assisted to heal from the hurts that they have endured, possibly in book two?

For now, please savour the characters and storylines that Pamela has created and her baby for which she allowed me to be her midwife.

Marcia M Spence ~ Book Development Strategist

Loving the Brothers
Pamela R Haynes

Editorial & Design Co-ordination: Marcia M Spence
Cover Design: Kevin Williams, Frank Image Ltd
Creative and Developmental Editor: Dawn Spence-Lewis
Revisions 2019 Susan Brookes Morris
Assisted by
R. Spence-Cork, S. Harvey, L. Mooruth, G. Forrester

Marcia M Publishing House
Empowering Writers to become Published Authors
marciampublishing.com

Printed in Great Britain
by Amazon